A Gathering in Hope

ALSO BY PHILIP GULLEY

A Place Called Hope
A Lesson in Hope

Available from Center Street wherever books are sold.

A Gathering in Hope

A Novel

PHILIP GULLEY

CENTER
STREET

New York Boston Nashville

Copyright © 2016 by Philip Gulley

Cover design by Jody Waldrup
Cover illustration by Robin Moline
Cover copyright © 2016 by Hachette Book Group, Inc.

Center Street
Hachette Book Group
1290 Avenue of the Americas
New York, NY 10104
centerstreet.com
twitter.com/centerstreet

First Edition: September 2016

Center Street is a division of Hachette Book Group, Inc.
The Center Street name and logo are trademarks of Hachette Book Group, Inc.

The publisher is not responsible for websites (or their content) that are not owned by the publisher.

The Hachette Speakers Bureau provides a wide range of authors for speaking events. To find out more, go to www.HachetteSpeakersBureau.com or call (866) 376-6591.

Library of Congress Cataloging-in-Publication Data
Names: Gulley, Philip, author.
Title: A gathering in Hope : a novel / Philip Gulley.
Description: New York : Center Street, 2016. | Series: Hope ; 3
Identifiers: LCCN 2016015453| ISBN 9781455562596 (hardcover) | ISBN 9781455519835 (ebook)
Subjects: LCSH: Clergy—Fiction. | Churches—Indiana—Fiction. | City and town life—Indiana—Fiction. | BISAC: FICTION / Humorous. | FICTION / Family Life. | FICTION / Christian / General. | GSAFD: Humorous fiction. | Christian fiction.
Classification: LCC PS3557.U449 G38 2016 | DDC 813/.54—dc23 LC record available at https://lccn.loc.gov/2016015453.

ISBN 978-1-4555-6259-6 (hardcover); 978-1-4555-1983-5 (ebook)

Printed in the United States of America

RRD-C

10 9 8 7 6 5 4 3 2 1

To Joan

Acknowledgments

With many thanks to my editor at Center Street, Christina Boys, and my agents, Steve Hanselman of Level Five Media and Stacey Denny of GraceTalks.

A Gathering in Hope

1

Sam Gardner lay awake, unable to sleep for the snoring of Wayne Newby, slumbering in their guest bedroom. Since Wayne had moved in, Sam caught himself wishing he'd never heard of God, and thus had never become a Quaker pastor, and consequently had never invited Wayne Newby to live with them when his wife, Doreen, had kicked him to the curb.

"How can one man make so much noise?" Sam's wife, Barbara, asked.

"Because he's overweight and has sleep apnea and refuses to do anything about it," Sam answered. "That's what we're hearing, the vibration of neck fat."

"I never knew fat could be so noisy."

"He's out of here today," Sam said. "Doreen said he could come home."

Several months before, Doreen had found a girlie magazine in Wayne's workbench and in a fit of indignation had ordered Wayne from their home. Sam had invited him to stay for what he thought would be one night, but that was months ago, and Wayne was still camped out in their guest bedroom, making himself more at home each passing day. He had shed all modesty and would walk around in their home in his underwear, scratching his gut. Winter had passed and spring was upon them, the season of romance, which Sam and Barbara could not celebrate, given Wayne's tendency of walking into their bedroom unannounced. Barbara changed clothes in the closet and slept in sweat pants, which was hardly conducive to passion.

But this morning, Wayne would depart for his own home, chastened and repentant, having learned his lesson, or so he had promised Doreen.

Sam had a church meeting that night, which he hoped would end early, though one never knew with Quakers, who were prone to getting worked up, stretching a one-hour meeting to four or five hours.

Barbara rolled over and draped her leg across Sam. "What time will you be home from your meeting tonight?" she asked, her voice low and husky.

"Eight o'clock at the latest," Sam said. "It's a trustee meeting. It shouldn't last that long."

Hank Withers was the new clerk of the trustees, and was wielding his significant power to see a new kitchen and fellowship room built, the meeting having received an inheritance from the estate of Olive Charles, who no one thought had a dime to her name, but turned out to be loaded, and croaked, leaving her beloved Quaker meeting a wad of cash, a house, and a 1979 Ford Granada. They had been bickering ever since, the majority of the congregation wanting to build on, while Wanda and Leonard Fink were holding out for a sizable donation to Wanda's nephew who had left the comforts of home to minister to the lost souls of Norway, who were numerous according to the letters he sent his aunt Wanda. Lost and de-praved and bound for hell. He wasn't sure how much longer he could stay in Norway. He was under spiritual attack, sur-rounded by Norwegians who scoffed at the Lord, having put their faith in socialized medicine and all other manner of evil.

Sam was well into his second year as the pastor of Hope Friends Meeting and had been fervently praying Wanda and Leonard Fink would leave, but they hung on like a nasty virus that left one nauseous and worn-out. They had been against Sam from the start, opposed to his coming to Hope, after learning he had inadvertently performed a same-gender mar-riage at his previous church, Harmony Friends Meeting. He had married two women, Chris and Kelly, who, given their names, could have been any gender, so how was Sam supposed to know they were both women when he agreed over the phone to perform their wedding? By the time he discovered the truth, he was halfway through the ceremony and couldn't very well stop, so he plunged ahead and was summarily fired. The Quakers in Harmony would have executed him had the law permitted it, so the firing showed considerable restraint.

He had been the pastor of Harmony for fourteen years, and had grown up there to boot, which apparently counted for nothing. His grandmother and mother had made miles of noodles for the Friendly Women's Circle and still he had been tossed aside like yesterday's newspaper. He had taken the only church that would have him, a Quaker meeting of a dozen souls, and after working his tail off had boosted their number to nearly thirty. Thirty mostly wonderful, al-beit quirky, people—save for the Finks, who were oblivious to Sam's hints that they might be happier at the Baptist church down the street.

But Sam put all of that out of his mind. Wayne Newby was finally going home, and he and Barbara would be alone again, just the two of them, with only a trustee meeting standing between them and romance. The three of them ate breakfast, Barbara left for her library job at the school, then Sam helped Wayne load his truck, and waved good-bye as Wayne backed out of their driveway and drove down the meeting-house lane, and out of Sam's life, at least until that evening's trustee meeting.

2

⌒

It was a Monday, a bright blue spring day, Sam's day off, and
he had no plans. The best kind of day. He tinkered in the
yard all morning, raking the winter debris from around the
house, and hauling it to the compost pile in back of the meetinghouse. A Quaker meeting with even one leftover hippie
could be counted upon to have a compost pile. Barbara Gardner had begun theirs, over the objections of the Finks, who
said compost wasn't mentioned in the Bible and seemed suspi-
ciously close to reincarnation, turning one thing into another.
The clerk of the meeting, Ruby Hopper, had suggested they
take a month to pray about it, but Barbara had begun the compost pile anyway. It was warm and earthy and Sam loved the
smell of it. He liked the principle of it, too, that something use-
less could be made useful. Compost, in Sam's mind, had a
Jesus feel to it.

At noon, he knocked off for lunch, riding his bicycle to
Bruno's for lunch. At first, he hadn't cared for Bruno, who
had given every indication of wanting to kill him so he could
run off with Barbara, but over time they had become friends

and Sam was a frequent diner. Ravioli with a side salad and garlic roll. If no church members were present, Bruno would bring him a dollop of red wine, which Sam drank for medicinal purposes.

"Do you still have your houseguest?" Bruno asked, sitting across from Sam.

"Nope, he left this morning. We have the house to ourselves now."

Bruno wriggled his eyebrows. "Ah, and it's springtime, the season for love."

Sam changed the subject. Italians were forthright about romance, which embarrassed Sam, having been taught such things were private matters, and perhaps even sinful, depending on how much one enjoyed it.

"Your wife, she's a beautiful woman," Bruno persisted. "She has a fire inside of her, I can tell."

"So when are you going to come visit our Quaker meeting?" Sam asked. "You keep saying you're going to drop in one Sunday, but you never do." Sam had discovered long ago that inviting people to church was the quickest way to be shed of them.

"How about a little wine?" Bruno asked, rising to his feet.

"No thank you. I need to keep my wits about me. I have a church meeting tonight."

"The life of a pastor," Bruno said. "Your time is not your own."

"I could be summoned any moment for an emergency," Sam agreed soberly. "Someone could die from a heart attack, a woman could discover her husband had cheated on her, a house might burn to the ground, and I'd have to help. That's when people call their pastor."

"Which husband cheated on his wife?" Bruno asked.

"I'm not saying anyone did, but if they did, the wife would call me once she found out."

"No, she wouldn't. Not these days. These days she'd go on one of those TV shows and slap her husband around in front of everyone."

"You're probably right there," Sam admitted.

"It's all changed from when I was a kid," Bruno said.

"No one calls their pastor anymore. Sometimes my phone doesn't ring the entire day," Sam confessed, rather glumly. "Now they just post their problems on Facebook."

Sam hated Facebook with a white-hot intensity. At first, he'd enjoyed it, then it had been taken over by whiners, kooks, and clods. When it started, he'd used it to contact old classmates, but then he remembered why he'd lost touch with them in the first place.

"My grandkids are all the time telling me to get on Facebook," Bruno said. "They say that way we can talk. Whatever happened to people visiting someone in their home?"

Sam lingered a bit longer, enjoying their mutual distaste for modern life, paid his bill, and went to Riggle's Hardware to discuss pocketknives, then crossed the street to Drooger's and bought a gallon of milk and a box of Cocoa Krispies. After a year of living in Hope, he was starting to know the cashier at Drooger's, a sweet, older woman named Mary Ann, who warned Sam about Cocoa Krispies. "That stuff will kill you. Just look at the ingredients. Alpha tocopherol acetate. What in the world is that? Don't they put acetate in paint? You don't want that stuff in your body. It's addictive, you know."

Sam assured Mary Ann he wasn't addicted, that he could quit anytime, and thanked her for her concern.

"I just worry about you is all. You remind me of my son. I nearly lost him, you know. He got hooked on Peeps and it threw his blood sugar out of whack and he almost died."

"I remember you telling me that," Sam said. "I hope Mike's doing better."

"He's better now, but it was touch and go for a while. He went through withdrawal. You can't eat five packages of Peeps a day for thirty years and then quit cold turkey. You got to wean yourself off them." She leaned closer to Sam and lowered her voice to a whisper. "Besides, you wouldn't believe the markup on cereal. It's a rip-off. You're better off with oats, trust me. Plus, you're a Quaker. Stick with your own kind."

Sam returned the Cocoa Krispies back to the shelf, and bought oats instead.

"This is the start of a new life for you," Mary Ann said, patting his hand. "I'm so proud of you."

He pedaled his bike home, steering with one hand, carrying his groceries in the other. He felt funny, a little jittery, and decided he was going through withdrawal, so took a nap and woke up just as Barbara was pulling into the driveway, home from her job. He hurried to the closet, pulled out the vacuum cleaner, plugged it in and began vacuuming the living room, looking frantically busy when she walked in the house. Timing, he had learned after thirty-some years of marriage, was everything.

3

ank Withers had quietly drawn the plans for a new addition to the Hope meetinghouse. He spent Monday afternoon consulting with a builder, trying to get an idea how much a new kitchen and fellowship hall might cost, which turned out to be considerably more than he had thought.

"It's those wooden beams and stone that are killing us," the builder said. "Don't get me wrong, it's a beautiful design, but if we go with wood veneers it'll be a lot cheaper. And they make this composite stone material, and you can't even tell it's not real."

"It's the genuine article or nothing," Hank said. "I've never designed something using fake materials and I'm not going to start now."

"Then you're going to have to come up with another three hundred thousand dollars," the builder said, "because I've trimmed all the fat off this estimate."

The builder had purposely estimated high, hoping the church would give the job to someone else. He hated working for churches, with all their committee meetings and last-

minute changes and a dozen people, none of whom understood the principles of building, bossing him around, ordering
him to do a dozen different things. Just the year before, while
building a church, he hadn't been told they wanted a baptismal
the floor couldn't support. One thousand gallons of water
at 8.3 pounds a gallon, plus a pastor who tipped the scales
at nearly three hundred pounds. Eight thousand six hundred
pounds that would crash through to the basement the first
time they filled it and old lard butt stepped in to baptize someone. He advised them to sprinkle instead of dunk, both sides
had lawyered up, and it was a mess.

"You don't want a baptismal added, do you?" he asked
Hank. "Tell me now if you do, so I can plan for it."

"Quakers don't do water baptisms," Hank said. "We dry-
clean."

"Well, that'll save you some money."

Building a fellowship hall and kitchen had been Hank's
idea, motivated by the demise of Olive Charles, whom he was
confident would have been in favor of the idea had she lived
long enough to voice her opinion on the matter.

"So when did your church want to break ground?" the
builder asked Hank.

"Give me another month to get things in order, then we'll
be ready." The fact that Hope Meeting hadn't yet decided to
build was a small stumbling block, but something Hank didn't
think should stand in the way of progress.

The builder left Hank his business card, promised to take
another look at the bid to see if he could trim it down, then
left. Hank followed him out the driveway, his mind preoccupied with that night's trustee meeting. Leonard Fink had
re-upped for another term on the trustees and was dead-set

against building. His wife, Wanda, was bound and determined to see the money spent on getting people saved before God killed them dead and pitched them in hell where they belonged.

Hank was pretty sure Wayne Newby wanted to build, and he knew Sam could be talked into it, especially if they used part of the inheritance to give him a raise. But Wilson Roberts could go either way. If he agreed to build, it was a done deal, since the Finks would be the only ones opposed and no one liked them, not even Jesus. But people respected Wilson Roberts, so if he held back, then Ruby Hopper wasn't likely to approve building and if Ruby didn't go for it, then neither would Ellen Hadley, who clerked the pie committee and thus wielded considerable power in the congregation.

Ellen Hadley aggravated Hank Withers to no end. She didn't even come to church, he hadn't seen her in months, but she had her hand in everything. The thing about Ellen Hadley is that people actually liked her, on account of the pies. She had baked pies for a church fund-raiser, then had kept right on baking, bringing pies to church every Sunday until people were hooked, until they would do anything for a pie, including starting a brand-new pie committee and putting her in charge of it. She had Ruby Hopper, who was normally sensible, baking the pies, and now those Quakers were addicted, craving their next fix.

He had promised Ruby and Ellen a commercial pastry oven for the new meetinghouse kitchen, stainless steel, it could bake twenty pies at a time, and he sensed they were turning his way. They had been talking about using the money to help the poor, but were starting to waver. So Hank had thrown in a pie press. No more rolling out the dough, he told them. Toss the dough in a pan, the press came down, and *voila!*, a perfect pie crust every time. It's what Olive would have wanted. They'd think about it, they told him. But they were weakening, Hank could tell. If he could get Wilson on board, the addition was as good as built.

4

Wilson Roberts arrived early to the trustee meeting, at Hank's request. The drawings were rolled out on the folding table.

"Don't tell anyone I'm letting you see them," Hank said. "But I wanted to run them past you first, given your knowledge of these things."

"I understand," Wilson said, completely charmed. "We don't want people who don't know anything about building shooting this down."

Hank thrilled at the word *we*.

"Has Sam seen these yet?" Wilson asked.

"No, not yet. I wanted you to see them first."

"We've got to get Sam on our side," Wilson said. "Something tells me he might not want to see all this money spent on a building. He's got a liberal streak in him and you know how liberals can be."

"Oh, I think Sam's with us," Hank said. "Pastors love building additions."

They studied the drawings, Wilson made a change or two to

the restrooms. "You want these stall doors to swing out, not in. You get a big person in a stall with a door that swings in and they get trapped in there," he pointed out to Hank.

"Good catch."

"And if it were up to me, I'd make these urinals waterless," Wilson said. "They cost a little more up front, but save a lot of money and water in the long run."

"I was thinking the exact same thing," said Hank, who up until that moment had never heard of waterless urinals.

Hank rolled up the plans and stowed them in his car before the other trustees arrived—Wayne Newby, Leonard Fink, Dan Woodrum, and Sam.

Hank asked Sam if he would mind offering a prayer, and Sam did, thanking the Lord for items of interest to the trustees, up to and including power tools and paint and roofing shingles. He asked the Lord to bless the hands who had prepared the tools and building materials, to make them strong and healthy, then asked God to bless those who didn't have power tools or building materials. He closed his prayer with a hearty *amen*.

"I don't believe I've ever heard a prayer for building materials," Hank said. "Thank you, Sam. That was very nice."

Hank passed out the agenda, then called everyone's attention to the first item—changing the paper towel brand in the meetinghouse restrooms. He had found a different supplier that would save them twenty dollars a year; did the trustees approve switching the brand?

"I hate to see us invest in an entire carton of paper towels we haven't tried," Leonard Fink said. "If we don't like them, we're stuck. Maybe we should start with one package and ask folks how they like them."

"Or maybe have a stack of the new towels and a stack of the old ones, and ask people to try them both to see which they prefer," Wayne Newby added.

They discussed the merits of Wayne's suggestion for a half hour, going back and forth, pulling and pushing, straining for truth in this existential dilemma. Hank checked out. It was times like this, he hoped the meeting didn't build. If they spent a half hour discussing paper towels, building a new fellowship hall would take decades. Jesus would return before the first nail had been driven.

In the end, they thought it best not to change paper towel brands, and moved on to the second item, a discussion of whether or not to hire a janitor. The members had been taking turns cleaning the meetinghouse, but some took it more seriously than others, some forgot altogether, and it wasn't unusual to find old bulletins in the pews, dirty floors, and smudged glass.

"Not to get personal," Leonard Fink said, turning toward Wayne Newby, "but it was your job this past Christmas and the place was a dump."

"For crying out, I had a broken leg," Wayne said. "You don't expect me to clean this place with a broken leg, do you? I could barely walk."

"This is why we need a janitor," Hank said. "These things happen. It doesn't always work for everyone to be able to clean when it's their turn."

"I'm against it," Leonard said. "It's a waste of money when we can do it ourselves."

"But we can't do it ourselves, that's my point," Hank said. "We're all getting older and these things are going to be happening more and more to us."

"When I was growing up, the pastor cleaned the meeting-house," Leonard Fink said. "Sam's still young. Why can't he do it?"

"I'd rather not," Sam said. "I don't mind taking my turn, but I didn't go to college and graduate school eight years in order to be the janitor of a church."

"Pastors are supposed to be servants, first and foremost," Leonard said.

"I work a certain number of hours a week," Sam pointed out. "It's much more expensive for the meeting to pay me to clean than it would be to pay a janitor."

"Sam's got a point," Hank said.

"Why would you consider it part of your job?" Leonard asked. "We don't consider it part of our jobs. We're all volunteers here. Why can't you volunteer to clean the meeting-house?"

"Because cleaning isn't my spiritual gift," Sam said. "You can ask Barbara. She'll tell you that."

"For Pete's sake, we just inherited a million dollars. Let's hire someone to come in a couple hours a week and clean the meetinghouse," Wilson Roberts said. "It won't cost us more than a hundred dollars."

"In that case, Wanda and I would be happy to serve as the new janitors," Leonard Fink said smugly, leaning back in his chair, his arms crossed, handily checkmating the committee.

Slick, Hank thought. He had to hand it to Leonard. Very slick.

5

The trustees looked at one another, aware they'd been hoodwinked, mad at themselves, and not quite ready to surrender.

"We probably shouldn't hire a member," Hank Withers said. "It could cause trouble if there were a misunderstanding."

Leonard leaned forward. "We hired Sam and he's a member of the meeting," he said.

"It's different, he's our pastor," Wilson Roberts said. "Of course he's a member."

"So our pastor can be a member of the meeting, but not our janitor? That doesn't seem fair," Leonard said. "I thought Quakers believed in equality."

"How do Friends feel about that?" Hank asked the other trustees. "Are you comfortable with the meeting hiring Leonard and Wanda to clean the meetinghouse for seventy-five dollars a week?"

"I thought it was a hundred," Leonard said.

"Okay, a hundred," Hank agreed. "Do Friends approve?"

"Approved," they rumbled, except for Sam, who was mortified at the prospect of Leonard and Wanda Fink hanging around the meetinghouse while he was trying to work.

"Then let's move on," Hank said. "Next item. Our new addition. We need to make a recommendation to the church to build it. It's just a formality, but it needs to be done. Are you comfortable with me bringing that to the church?"

"Hold your horses," Leonard Fink said. "We haven't agreed that we even need an addition."

Hank began leafing through the minutes from past meetings. "I'm looking at the notes from our February ninth meeting. It says here that I'm supposed to draw up plans for an addition. Everyone approved."

"That's not the same as building it," Leonard said. "We haven't even seen the plans."

"I was going to show them to everyone in the church at once," Hank said.

"Trustees ought to get to see them first," Leonard said.

"I think we need to name a brand-new committee, a building committee," Wayne Newby suggested.

Oh, Lord, no, Sam thought. *Not another committee. Please, Lord, not another committee.*

"I like that idea," Hank said. "We need some focused attention on this matter."

"How can we have a committee for a building we've not even agreed to build?" Leonard snapped.

"Just in case," Hank said smoothly. "If the meeting decides to do it, then we can hit the ground running."

"Wanda and I are opposed to this and have been from the start. And we're not the only ones. I've heard from others who aren't happy about it, either," Leonard said.

"What others?" Hank asked.

"I told 'em I wouldn't tell their names," Leonard said.

Ah, Sam thought, *the mysterious others, the anonymous others, who complain to everyone except the people involved.*

"We're not playing that game," Hank said. "If people don't want to do it, they should speak up and say so. None of this 'others' stuff."

Wilson Roberts leaned back in his chair. "Back in the olden days, if Quakers had something they couldn't agree on, they appointed a committee to help the meeting decide the Lord's will. They called them clearness committees. Why don't we form a clearness committee, so it can help us decide whether or not to build?"

Two committees formed in the space of one minute, which had to be a record, even among the Quakers.

6

Chris and Kelly Johnson, now happily and legally married in the state of Indiana, were packing up their kitchen, sorting their dishes into two stacks—keep and Goodwill. After a year's search, they had landed jobs in the city, so were leaving Cartersburg. People from their church, the Unitarians in Harmony, were helping them move. Chris and Kelly, being the first same-gender couple in the vicinity to wed, were something of a curiosity, people not yet accustomed to two women being married to one another. The locals had questions they wanted to ask, but didn't for the sake of good manners. Questions like, "Who mows the lawn?" and "Which one of you does the cooking?" Duties they believed God had assigned to specific genders that had to be reconsidered in a same-gender marriage. The big question, of course, that everyone felt quite free to ask, was, "Whose last name will you take?" Kelly had taken Chris's last name, her maiden name being Dorf and something she'd wanted to shed as long as she could remember.

The Unitarians dribbled in throughout Saturday morning,

carrying furniture and boxes to the U-Haul, then gathered in the driveway to wish Chris and Kelly every success in their venture. Pastor Matt asked the Great Spirit to bless their endeavors, then said, "Your new house is very near Sam Gardner's Quaker meeting. If you see him, give him our best."

Matt had been kept up to date on the goings-on at Hope Friends Meeting by his girlfriend Janet Woodrum, whose parents, Dan and Libby, attended the meeting.

"Yes, we know," Chris said. "We were thinking of visiting Sam's church."

"But only if it won't get him in trouble," Kelly added. "He lost his job here because of us. We don't want to make things bad for him."

"Janet told me Hope Meeting is more open," Matt said. "I think he'd be delighted to see you."

Chris and Kelly hugged everyone good-bye, climbed in the U-Haul, and drove west out of town, toward the interstate. The traffic was light, they stopped for a late lunch, and rolled into Hope in the late afternoon. Kelly studied her cell phone, guiding Chris through the streets of Hope to their new home, which turned out to be three blocks from the meetinghouse. Their parents and siblings were already there, ready to help them carry in their belongings and unpack them. Box after box, chairs, tables, and clothing, Kelly directing what went where. Within a few hours they were finished and took everyone to Bruno's for dinner. It had been a wonderful day, their future was bright, and the world was their oyster.

7

Sam had been depressed since Monday night's trustee meeting. He had gone online and read that 90 percent of pastors involved in building programs were fired or left within two years. There was a website for pastors canned because of building projects, so he read a few of the stories. They were bloodbaths—pastors sacked in the middle of worship services, pastors kicked out of the parsonage with a day's notice. Horrible, chilling stories that made him wonder why any pastor would undertake a building program. His cell phone had been vibrating since Tuesday morning with everyone calling to offer their opinion on the subject of building. Finally, on Saturday, Barbara had made Sam take their phone off the hook and turn off his cell phone. They were at Bruno's, deciding whether to have dessert, when Sam nudged Barbara.

"Do you know those people?" he asked, pointing discreetly at another table. "Those women look familiar."

"I've never seen them," she said.

He studied them carefully, unable to place them. He was not only bad with names, he wasn't too sharp with faces.

Across the room, Mrs. Dorf leaned over to her daughter Kelly, subtly gesturing toward Sam. "Isn't that the minister who married you kids?"

Kelly glanced at Sam, recognized him immediately, took Chris by the hand, and walked across the restaurant to greet him. "Sam, what a pleasure to see you," Kelly said. "Do you remember us?"

Sam hated it when people asked if he remembered them, especially if they were attractive women and his wife was with him. "You do look familiar to me. Did we meet at Riggle's Hardware?"

Chris chuckled. "No, we met at the Unitarian church in Harmony. You performed our wedding, remember?"

"Oh, sure, now I remember," said Sam, as if marrying lesbians were an everyday occurrence. "What brings you to Hope?"

"We've just moved here," Kelly said. "We found jobs in the city. Matt told us you lived here, and said to tell you hello if we saw you, but we didn't count on seeing you so soon."

"I don't believe you've met my wife; this is Barbara. Honey, this is, uh—"

Chris reached out to shake Barbara's hand. "I'm Chris Johnson and this is my wife, Kelly."

"Very nice to meet both of you," Barbara said. "When did you move here?"

"About three hours ago," Kelly said.

"Then let us be the first to welcome you to Hope," Barbara said. "It's a wonderful community."

"We've heard good things," Kelly said. "Of course, we're still finding our way around."

"If you're looking for a church home, you're welcome to visit Hope Friends," Barbara said.

Sam had recently noticed Barbara's willingness to invite people to church, now that she belonged to a church where newcomers wouldn't be buttonholed by Dale Hinshaw and asked if they were saved, or when they thought the Lord would return, or whether they were presently Communists, or ever had been.

"We were talking about churches on the way up," Chris said. "The Unitarian church is on the other side of the city. When Matt told us you were here, we thought we'd visit your meeting."

"You're more than welcome. Meeting for worship begins at ten thirty," Barbara said. She gave them directions to the meetinghouse, Sam mentioned the pies, and they promised to visit once they were settled.

They chatted a bit longer, then Kelly and Chris excused themselves and returned to their families, while Sam and Barbara decided on a dessert, which Sam couldn't pronounce, but was delicious nonetheless.

8

Sam and Barbara, having stuffed themselves, went the long way home, walking hand in hand underneath the streetlights that were just starting to flicker on. They stopped to visit his parents, who had moved to Hope to be closer to Sam and his brother, Roger, who had also moved to Hope, having purchased Olive Charles's old home with his girlfriend Christina Pringle. Christina and Roger were on the cusp of marriage, they were working on a date, which would move Christina's father, Otis Pringle, into the relative category, something Sam had hoped to avoid. Otis Pringle, a fellow Quaker minister, knew a little too much about God to suit Sam. He had been talking about retiring and moving to Hope and helping Sam with his ministry, even though Sam hadn't asked for help. Sam had been praying Otis would suddenly, painlessly die before he could move to Hope. Or maybe Otis would perish while saving a baby from a house fire and be covered with glory and have a statue made of him and erected at the Quaker headquarters, which Otis would love, having always believed a statue was his due.

Christina Pringle was nothing like her father. She was beautiful and intelligent and good-humored and a doctor, for crying out loud. Sam was still trying to figure out how his doofus of a brother had landed Christina. For the past twenty years, Roger had dated a series of oddballs—vegans and Goths and women who slept in trees to keep them from being cut down—then had gone online and found Christina on a Quaker dating site. She didn't look like any Quaker Sam had ever met.

Roger and Christina were at his parents' house, sitting at the kitchen table eating supper.

"We'd invite you to eat, but we don't have enough," Sam's mother, Gloria Gardner, said. "We forgot to invite you."

Forgot to invite him? How could his own mother forget to invite him? She had two sons, both of whom lived two minutes away and saw her every day. Forget him?

"That's okay, Mom. We ate at Bruno's," Sam said.

Forgot him?

"Say, Sam, I've decided these wood floors need to be sanded," his father said. "Can you give me next week?"

"Sorry, Dad, I have to work. Why don't you call Hank Withers and see if he knows someone you can hire?"

Charles Gardner never hired anyone to do anything, except in the rarest of circumstances. Ten years ago, he'd needed an operation for a hernia and had contemplated doing it himself. "How hard can it be?" he'd said to his wife. "You make an incision, push the intestine back in, sew up the abdominal wall, close things up, and you're done. A sharp knife, some thread, and a needle is all it takes. In and out in fifteen minutes."

He'd read a story in a magazine about a doctor who'd operated on herself at the South Pole. That he wasn't a doctor was no impediment at all. "It's no different than skinnin' a squirrel," he'd told Gloria. He'd had his shirt off, and a knife in his hand, ready to cut, when Gloria called Sam, who ran over, disarmed his father, then drove him to the doctor's in Cartersburg, who had charged Charles Gardner six thousand dollars to do something he was perfectly capable of doing himself. He was livid, and hadn't seen a doctor since. Now he'd bought an old house and was killing himself fixing it up and would probably drop dead of a heart attack or fall off the roof or get lead poisoning. Sam had caught him melting lead fishing weights and mixing it into the paint. It was a wonder Charles Gardner was still alive. When he wasn't working on the house, he was racked out on the couch, snoring away, which he seemed to be doing more and more lately. Probably laid out from lead poisoning.

It gave Sam a headache to spend much time at his parents' house. He thought it was maybe the lead, or his father, one or the other, so after a half hour he and Barbara excused themselves and walked home. Turning down the meetinghouse lane, Barbara pointed out the Big Dipper above the trees. Sam lined up the two stars of the Dipper's edge, found the Little Dipper, and traced down its handle to the North Star. He turned and pointed south toward Georgia. "That's where Addison is," he said. Their youngest son had joined the army after high school. A kind, thoughtful boy who had come of age after 9/11 and wanted to help his country, he was now an army medic, serving in Georgia, which was almost like a foreign country. They talked with him every Sunday evening, but it wasn't the same as seeing him. If Sam thought about it too long, it made him sad, so he thought of spring instead and how the song of summer was just ahead.

9

You don't suppose they'll come to meeting, do you?" Sam asked Barbara. They were lying in bed, the lights were out, and Sam was thinking over his day.

"Don't suppose who will come to meeting?"

"Chris and Kelly? You don't really think they'll show up, do you?"

"They seemed interested," Barbara said. "I hope they come. They seem like really nice people."

"I don't know if the meeting is ready for a same-gender couple," Sam said. "I don't think the Finks will like it."

"Who cares what the Finks like," Barbara said. "Maybe if they don't like it enough, they'll leave."

"And go straight to the superintendent and complain about me," Sam said.

"What do you care what the superintendent thinks of you. He doesn't even like you," Barbara said.

"You don't have to be so blunt about it," Sam said. "He might like me."

"Oh, for crying out loud, you don't even respect him. Why would you care whether or not he liked you?"

"Everyone wants to be liked," Sam said. "Even by people they don't like."

Sam was ten years away from retirement, and Barbara didn't think she could make it. His anxieties were wearing thin. She had hoped he would become less neurotic as he aged, but he showed no sign of letting up. He spent most of his waking hours fretting about things that never happened—the entire church getting mad and quitting, Jesus returning on the clouds and finding him at the Dairy Queen engaged in gluttony, one of the seven deadly sins.

"Sam, if they show up, they show up. If they don't, they don't. The world won't end either way. Just relax and go to sleep."

Hank Withers had stopped by the meetinghouse that morning when Sam was copying the Sunday bulletin. He'd shown Sam the plans for the addition and told Sam he was ready for battle. Had said it just like that. Ready for battle. Sam's stomach had hurt ever since. Sam hadn't told Barbara, but he phoned Ruby Hopper, the clerk of the meeting, to express his concern.

"The Finks called me this week," Ruby had told him. "They're adamant about not building. And they said they weren't the only ones."

"Did they tell you who else was against it?" Sam had asked.

"Apparently Doreen Newby is opposed to building. I spoke with her about it. She's worried we won't have enough money to maintain it."

"Perhaps we can set aside part of the money in an account for future maintenance," Sam suggested.

"Hank said it's going to take every dime we have, possibly more, to build the addition."

On that cheerful note, their conversation had ended, though the topic had remained uppermost in Sam's mind through the day. They hadn't spent the first dime of Olive's inheritance and it already wasn't enough. Times like this, the prospect of being fired didn't sound all that bad.

When he finally fell asleep, he dreamed they built the addition and their little Quaker meeting grew exponentially, with hundreds of new people joining every year, more than Sam could keep track of. Then one Sunday morning, he couldn't find his clothes and had to preach in the nude, a hymnal covering his vitals. He awoke in a panic, looking around frantically, exhausted by his dream. He wondered if the dream was a message, a portent of things to come, a sign of future humiliations.

Fortunately, this Sunday morning, he found his clothes in his closet, right where he had hung them. He might well embarrass himself today, but at least he would be clothed when he did it.

10

Herb and Stacey Maxwell were fed up with their church, absolutely, unequivocally fed up. The Sunday before the pastor had pulled them aside after worship, pointed out their giving had declined, and said he wouldn't be responsible if God decided to smite them for their unfaithfulness.

"Remember when you encouraged Stacey to stay home after the twins were born? You said a mother's place was in the home. Well, she quit her job and now we don't make as much money," Herb pointed out. "Of course our giving is down."

"You need to trust the Lord to provide," the minister said. "Sow your seed of faith and watch God multiply it a hundred times over."

They had decided to find another church instead, so had gone online and taken a test—twenty questions, the answers to which would determine the religion most likely to suit them. In their instance, a somewhat tiny Christian denomination, well past 350 years old, founded in England by a rather eccentric man named George Fox. And though Herb and Stacey weren't sure what Quakers believed, the test suggested they should give them a try.

"Isn't that a Quaker church down the street?" Herb asked Stacey. "We've met their pastor. Chatty guy, middle-aged, walks everywhere."

"Yes. Sam. His wife's name is Barbara," Stacey said. "You want to go there?"

"Might as well," Herb said, which is how they ended up at Hope Friends Meeting the next Sunday, each carrying one of the twins.

An infant had not crossed the meetinghouse threshold in living memory, and now there were two. The Quakers flocked around them, beside themselves with excitement.

"Those people look familiar," Sam whispered to Barbara. "Where do we know them from?"

"They live down the street. Herb and Stacey Maxwell. The babies are Ezra and Emma."

"Boy, they really hung it on their son," Sam whispered. "Why would someone name their boy Ezra? Do they think it's the eighteen hundreds?"

"Shhh, they'll hear you. Pipe down and go welcome them."

Sam crossed the room, his hand extended, and greeted the Maxwells. He shook Herb's hand, told Stacey it was a pleasure to see them, then slipped over to Dan and Libby Woodrum to draft them for nursery duty.

The Monday before, at the trustee meeting, Sam had suggested they freshen up the nursery, that the dust was an inch thick and needed to be cleaned in case someone showed up with a baby. The trustees, all of them old men, had launched into a discussion of the benefits of dust, that children today had allergies because everything was too clean.

"You take those Amish kids," Wilson Roberts had said, "they don't have nearly the allergies other kids do because they're in and out of barns and it toughens them up. What's in a barn? Dust! Dust and manure. It won't hurt a kid to inhale a little dust."

Sam had brought a can of Pledge and a dust rag over from the house the next morning and had cleaned it himself. Now he was glad he had. He introduced the Maxwells to the Woodrums, who offered to watch Ezra and Emma. Stacey had grown up in Hope, Libby Woodrum had been her third-grade teacher, so she happily handed over her twins. They walked into the nursery. It smelled of chemical lemons, but not bad for fake fruit. Ruby Hopper hurried in, booted Dan Woodrum out of the nursery, and took a twin in her arms.

"Isn't she just adorable?" Ruby Hopper said to Sam.

"That's a he," Stacey said. "We dress them in yellow so they can share clothes. Ezra has a tiny mole just above his eye. That's how you can tell them apart."

As bad a name as Ezra was, Sam was glad they hadn't named him Mole.

"How many children are in the church?" Stacey Maxwell asked.

Sam tried to think up a way to say *none* that didn't sound depressing. "Not many children," he said, "but lots of grandparents who'll love your children."

"It's important to us that our children have friends in the church," Stacey said.

"Oh, they'll have lots of friends," Sam promised. "Maybe not their own age, but they won't lack for company."

Besides, Sam thought, what did a baby care about having other babies around? It wasn't like they could go out for pizza or anything like that.

He introduced Herb to Hank Withers, who asked him what

he did. Sam hated when other men asked him what he did, given the common perception most men had of pastors. Killjoys, a momma's boy, a Nancy, he'd heard it all. Hank was an architect, which placed him high on the list of great guy-jobs, right after Navy SEAL and just before NASCAR driver. Sam had never told another guy he was a minister only to have the guy sigh and say, "Boy, I sure wish I could be a minister."

"I'm a doctor for the Colts," Herb said.

"This place is swarming with doctors," Hank Withers groused, sensing his rank within the meeting took a hit every time a doctor began attending.

"That would be a great job," Sam said, impressed.

"It's not as glamorous as it sounds," Herb said, lying through his teeth.

How could it not be glamorous? Sure, you had to put up with jock itch and pus and athlete's foot, but you got to stand on the sidelines during a game in the event a receiver didn't see the goalpost and ran into it, knocking himself silly.

"Who gives the cheerleaders their physicals?" Hank asked.

"I do that, too," Herb said. "All in a day's work."

The only thing he did on physical day was listen to the cheerleaders' hearts, and measure their pulse and blood pressure. They could have worn winter coats during the entire procedure, but he wasn't about to tell Hank Withers and Sam Gardner that.

Herb had been attending the meeting only ten minutes and had rocketed to the top of guy-job mountain. Hank slunk away, his tail between his legs, a male dog defeated.

11

Sam introduced the Maxwells to several Quakers, deftly steering them away from the Finks and Doreen Newby, who had lately become a bit unpredictable. Dan Woodrum invited Herb and Stacey to sit with him, and worship began. Sam preached about King David and Bathsheba, how David had spied Bathsheba taking a bath, how seeing her naked had driven David mad with lust. Halfway into his sermon Sam remembered that Herb Maxwell saw naked cheerleaders on a regular basis, so he quickly added that if seeing naked people was part of your job, then it was okay.

It had started out as a sermon on the importance of modesty and pure thoughts, but mentioning the word *naked* had caused people's minds to wander to naked people they had known. As for Sam, he thought there was too much nudity these days. Why couldn't people keep their clothes on? You couldn't even watch television anymore without being embarrassed, for crying out loud. Sam hadn't seen Barbara naked until their wedding night, and that was in the dark. They hadn't turned on the lights until their third year of marriage.

Then Barbara had taken a good look at him, and turned the lights back off.

Sam's sermons had lately been wandering afield, after he'd read an article on preaching without notes. The trick was to memorize key words, using the first letter of each word to form another word entirely, an acronym. Except he often forgot the acronym, then was reduced to rummaging around in the alphabet, looking for a stray letter that might jog his memory. Barbara had pleaded with him to use notes, but he had decided to give it one more try. Now he had the entire congregation thinking impure thoughts, wasn't sure how to clean up the mess, so decided to shut up and sit down.

They entered into silence. After a few moments, Wayne Newby stood and talked about how when he and Doreen were first married, there had been a physical intensity to their relationship that was no longer present, but that passion had given way to enduring love. Then Wayne realized he had revealed too much and wondered what in the world had possessed him to share such a thing in public. Doreen was staring daggers at him. Everyone else was repulsed, trying not to think of Wayne and Doreen Newby being physically intense. Sam was sorry he had raised the subject in the first place and decided then and there to start a new sermon series on the topic of church history, something safe and boring that wouldn't get folks all stirred up.

After worship, Ruby Hopper emerged from the nursery to serve pie, Sam's favorite part of the morning. She had made a coconut cream pie, just for him, which he reluctantly shared with others after Barbara whispered in his ear not to be a pig. He ate his pie, then gabbed with the twins, who couldn't talk back, though they did stare at him and Emma even smiled. He chatted with Stacey Maxwell and discovered she was a lawyer, which made him nervous. Lawyers, he had discovered in his long years of ministry, enjoyed matching their wits with the pastor, and pastors almost always lost. No one could argue better than a lawyer. He made a mental note not to discuss theology with her, which would be difficult, he being her pastor. Well, not exactly yet, but maybe if things worked out, if the Finks didn't do something stupid to send them packing.

People doing something stupid was the curse of pastors everywhere, who worked hard to attract thoughtful people, only to have some half-baked kook in the congregation run them off. Of course, that road ran two ways. Sometimes people in the church invited someone to attend, only to have an idiot minister chase them off. Sam wondered if a rule could be passed barring dim-witted people from attending church. He helped himself to another piece of pie, and sat thinking whether or not it would be Christian to make people pass a test before they joined the church.

12

~

Monday morning dawned bright and early, while Sam luxuriated in bed. The trees were alive with birds, and Barbara was cooking oatmeal for breakfast, weaning Sam from Cocoa Krispies. The peace was broken by loud knocking on their front door. Barbara hurried to answer it, and opened the door to find Wanda Fink standing in their doorway.

"We've come to clean the meetinghouse," she said. "Do you have any glass cleaner? We were out of it at home."

Sam glanced at the bedside clock. Six thirty.

"And I need to talk to Sam," he heard Wanda say.

"He's still in bed," Barbara answered.

"Can you wake him up and tell him we need the key to his office? We need to vacuum the carpet."

Vacuum the carpet, my foot, Sam thought. *She wants to snoop through my desk.*

"Sam's pretty particular about office privacy," he heard Barbara say. "He has confidential notes in there."

"How does he expect us to clean his office if he won't give us the key?" Wanda said.

"I don't expect you to clean my office," Sam yelled from the bedroom. "I'll clean it myself."

He wasn't letting the Finks within a mile of his office. They'd study the phone register to see who he'd called, and read the crumpled notes in his wastebasket. He reminded himself to buy a paper shredder.

"I think Drooger's is open. They sell glass cleaner," Barbara said. "Maybe you need to go there and get stocked up on cleaning supplies. I'm sure the trustees won't mind the expense."

"Boy, you'd think we were made of money, the way we're running through it," Wanda groused, then stomped off, her plans to snoop defeated.

The oatmeal was delicious. Brown sugar, raisins, with a dab of milk, plus three strips of bacon, and a glass of orange juice. They read the morning newspaper together, did the crossword puzzle to keep from getting Alzheimer's, then Barbara kissed him good-bye and left for work.

Sam showered and dressed, then headed over to the office. The Finks were still there, dabbing halfheartedly at the windows. He called out a greeting and hurried into his office, hoping to avoid a conversation. Leonard Fink scurried across the meetingroom and followed Sam into his office.

"I'll get your trash while I'm here," he said, picking up Sam's wastebasket.

He pulled scraps of paper from the trash, studying them, looking for juicy tidbits, or evidence of misconduct, perhaps a woman's name written in lipstick and a phone number. Something to get Sam fired.

Sam closed the door behind Leonard, turned on his computer, and began working on his next sermon, surfing the web for jokes about church history, which turned out to be in short supply. He wished he hadn't sent an e-mail to the congregation the night before announcing a new sermon series. Now he was stuck having to research the early church, something he wasn't the least bit interested in. Fortunately, no one in the meeting knew the first thing about church history, so he could make up a few exciting battle scenes, whip things up a bit, throw in a beheading or two, a random crucifixion here and there, make historic church councils more interesting than they had actually been.

Wanda Fink opened Sam's door to announce they were leaving. "We'll be back tomorrow," she said.

Sam wondered if the Finks were going to be an everyday event.

He wished he could go back in time to warn the early church leaders to be careful that their efforts didn't result in people like the Finks. Maybe build some correctives into the system, like un-baptisms. He thought of several people that needed un-baptizing. Line them up, rip the stripes from their sleeves like they did in old army movies, and give them the heave-ho. Though it was unlikely to happen, it was a pleasant thought nonetheless and put him in a good frame of mind for the day.

13

Herb and Stacey Maxwell had been discussing their morning at Hope Friends off and on for the past three days. They had been impressed by Ruby Hopper and Libby Woodrum, thought Hank Withers was a bit odd, and couldn't make up their minds about Sam, whose sermon about the dangers of nudity had struck them as strange.

"I've never heard a sermon quite like it," Stacey said. "It's like he didn't know where he was going with it."

"It was different," Herb agreed. "But he seems like a nice enough guy."

"Do you want to go back?"

"Let's give it one month," Herb suggested. "If we don't like it after a month, we'll try somewhere else."

"Fair enough."

"I might stay just for the pie," Herb said. "It was delicious."

"Does it bother you that there aren't any kids in the church?" Stacey asked.

"Not too much. I don't think it's because they don't like kids. They seemed happy to see ours. Maybe people just don't like all that silence."

"That's the part I liked the most," Stacey said. "It was so peaceful in there."

"It was, wasn't it. Our old church had so much noise. It's kind of nice to be able to sit quietly and think."

"Let's give it three months," Stacey said. "That way we'll get the real flavor of the place."

Herb nodded. "I can do three months."

The Maxwells had seen Sam and Barbara the night before, out for a walk in the neighborhood. They'd been out working in their yard and heard someone call their names, and there were the Gardners, coming up their driveway. They had thanked the Maxwells for visiting the meeting the Sunday before, chatted about the neighborhood, fussed over the twins, then had taken their leave.

It was the perfect pastoral visit, not too long, not too short, no hounding the Maxwells about religion, no pressing them to return, no bad-mouthing other churches, no dropping hints that they were thinking of building and could use some extra money.

Sam had started to tell the Maxwells about his new sermon series, but Barbara cut him off and asked about the twins.

"People don't want to hear about your next sermon series," Barbara told Sam when they were clear of the Maxwells. "It's not about you. Why do ministers think people are just sitting around wondering about upcoming sermons?"

Sam supposed she was right, and was discouraged by the thought. People gave plenty of thought to the next football game, they even talked about it on television. Just once, he'd like to hear a television commentator say, "This week at Hope Friends Meeting, Sam Gardner will be speaking about marriage equality. It promises to be an exciting morning. You'll remember that Gardner was fired from his previous Quaker meeting for conducting a same-gender marriage. Have enough people changed their mind on this topic? That's what Sam is betting on. We'll see if he's right. Join us at ten thirty this Sunday, then stay tuned afterward for a response from Franklin Graham."

"That's going to be an exciting morning, Chuck," the television cohost would say. "A lot of people have been looking forward to this matchup for a long time."

Then they would cut away to a video of Sam at his desk, deep in thought. People enjoying sermons as much as they did professional football, that would be something.

14

Something was happening at Hope Friends Meeting, something that made Sam both excited and anxious. He was seated on the facing bench looking at the congregation, studying the new people. Five new visitors this Sunday, many of them young. Herb and Stacey Maxwell were back with their twins; Chris and Kelly, the two women Sam had married, were present; and three others who had told Sam their names, which he had promptly forgot. One of the three, a young woman, had a ring through her right nostril. Sam had started to ask how she blew her nose, when Barbara, knowing exactly what he was about to do, introduced herself and steered the woman away from Sam so she could meet others.

After worship, they ate pie, then gathered for the monthly business meeting, something only the die-hard members attended. Ruby Hopper had no sooner prayed for God to be with them than Leonard Fink expressed his concern about certain people, he wouldn't mention names, coming to church with various body piercings, which needed to stop right now.

"Who's gonna tell her to take that ring out of her nose?" he demanded.

"Not me," Hank Withers said. "I don't care if she wears an arrow through her head. She's under twenty-five, and if you look around, we're not exactly overflowing with people that age."

"We never had people like that until Sam got here," Wanda Fink said.

"And who were those two women?" Leonard Fink asked. "Did you notice they were holding hands?"

Sam didn't volunteer their names. If Leonard wanted to know, he could ask them.

Ruby Hopper frowned. "Friends, it hardly behooves us to speak ill of others. We've been praying for God to send us people, and now they're coming and we should be grateful. Five new visitors just this morning. Not to mention the Maxwells and their beautiful babies. That's nine new people in two weeks."

"We need to get going on the new addition," Hank Withers said, never one to miss an opportunity to push for the building. "We're running out of room."

Doreen Newby frowned. "I'm not so sure adding on is a good idea. How are we going to afford to heat and maintain more space? And don't say the Lord will provide. I hate it when people say that."

"Well, we are a church," Wilson Roberts pointed out. "Aren't we supposed to have faith that God will provide?"

"Not when it's an excuse for bad planning," Leonard Fink said.

The headache began at the base of Sam's neck, where they always began, from tightening his shoulders. It arced across the top of his skull and settled between his eyes, piercing, throbbing. He got them once a month, at their business meetings. He marveled at Ruby Hopper, who could sit serenely hour after long hour, never raising her voice, never growing discouraged, never once plunging a knife into her eye to end the misery. Years before, Barbara had begun making Sam leave his pocketknife at home on the Sundays they had business meetings.

He sat squirming in his chair, wishing the meeting were over. If they did decide to build, an unbroken chain of meetings stretched before him. Meetings to pick the builder, meetings to pick the carpet, the paint, the windows, the doors, the trim. One meeting after another for the next several years. And he would be expected to attend every last one of them. If Quakers had the same retirement plan as the army, he could have retired ten years before, gotten a job at a hardware store, and never attended another meeting his entire life.

Wayne and Doreen Newby began squabbling about the building project. Wayne in favor, Doreen opposed, hissing at one another like snakes.

"I think we've discussed this matter enough for today," Ruby Hopper said. "Does anyone else have any new business items to discuss?"

"I've asked it once, I'll ask it again. Does Sam know those two women who were here today?" Leonard Fink said. "What can he tell us about them?"

Sam didn't answer.

"I don't think that's an appropriate question," Libby Woodrum said. "Whether Sam knows them or not doesn't matter. What matters is that they're here and we need to welcome them."

"I think they're lesbians," Wanda Fink said. "And if two show up, others will follow. You know how they are."

Yes, something was happening at Hope Friends Meeting, something that made Sam both excited and anxious, but mostly anxious.

15

Charles Gardner sat in his recliner, brooding, exhausted from Quaker meeting, where he'd been cornered by Hank Withers and asked to serve on the building committee. The chief reason he and his wife had moved to Hope was to get off the committees at Harmony Friends Meeting. They had told their sons, Sam and Roger, they'd moved to Hope to be closer to them, which was a bald lie. They had attended Harmony Meeting over fifty years, were thoroughly entrenched in the meeting, with no way to escape except leave town. Now they were in danger of becoming similarly imprisoned at Hope Meeting. Their fatal error had been joining the meeting, which had made them eligible to serve on committees.

"I don't want to serve on committees," he said to Gloria. "Even if our son is the pastor."

"Oh, it won't be all that hard. Hank seems like a take-charge kind of guy. It'll probably be built within a year and the committee will disband."

"Have you ever known a church committee to disband? Back in Harmony, we've kept the furnace committee going fifteen years after we bought the new furnace."

"This isn't Harmony. And if the committee does continue, you can always resign from it."

"I've got too much of my own work to do," Charles said, looking around the room. "I've still got to sand these floors, we need to paint, repair that drywall in the kitchen, upgrade the wiring in the basement. I don't have time to serve on a building committee. Why don't you serve on the building committee?"

"They didn't ask me," Gloria Gardner said.

"You can volunteer. They ought to have a couple women on that committee anyway. Especially since the plans include a new kitchen. You ever think what a kitchen designed by a bunch of old men would be like?"

"I hadn't thought of that," Gloria said, troubled at the prospect. "What a mess that would be."

"Then call Hank and volunteer to serve in my place," Charles said.

Hank was delighted to have her serve on the committee. The pastor's mother or father, he didn't care which, he just wanted someone on the committee related to Sam who could apply some artful pressure, should it be necessary. Get the minister under the thumb of the building committee and keep him there.

That morning, Hank had been able to nudge the meeting another inch down the road. They had consented to letting him interview potential builders, which he had already been doing anyway. Meeting at night in parking lots, wearing a fake mustache in case someone from the meeting saw him. He'd been meeting with a builder who had worked with churches in the past, but after spending a few hours with Hank, he had declined the job. Hank was settling on a builder who'd never worked with churches before and thus was hopelessly naïve. The man had actually told Hank he thought it might be *fun*. *Fun!* Hank had wanted to hire the man on the spot.

With further prodding, and over the Finks' strenuous objections, Hank had also gained approval to apply for a building permit, which he could use as a crowbar to pry the reluctant. Doreen Newby had pulled him aside after the meeting to ask whether building permits could be canceled if the church decided not to build.

"It pretty well commits us," he'd told her, lying with such ease he almost felt guilty. "Oh, I'm sure if we went to court and spent a lot of money on lawyers, we might be able to get out of it, but once the government issues a building permit it has the force of law."

"I had no idea."

"Yes, I once heard about a church that reneged on its building permit and all the trustees were arrested and thrown in jail. It's serious business."

Doreen's husband, Wayne, was a trustee, and while she'd had her issues with Wayne, she had no wish to see him imprisoned.

She'd had no idea the building process was so fraught with peril, and left the meetinghouse uneasy, wondering if the time had come for her to become a Methodist.

16

⌒⌒

On the first warm day of spring, Gloria Gardner, thirty pounds overweight and determined to lose it, had walked to Riggle's Hardware and purchased a bicycle. As a child, she'd enjoyed bicycling, but hadn't been on a bicycle since teaching Sam to ride, almost fifty years before. But once you learn to ride a bicycle, you never forget, as the saying goes, and when Charley Riggle wheeled the bike to the parking lot, helped her mount it, then pushed her off, she found her bicycling legs and was nine years old again, pedaling down the sidewalk toward home.

She stopped at Sam's house, where her son seemed somewhat startled by his mother's decision to take up bicycling in her late seventies.

"You don't even have a helmet," he pointed out. "If you wreck, you're a goner."

"Did you wear a helmet when you rode your bicycle everywhere?"

"Mom, that's not the point. They didn't even have helmets then. You need to protect your head. That's not all that could happen. What if you have a heart attack and die?"

"Sam, I'm almost eighty. My life is nearing its end. I'd rather die quickly on a bicycle than languish in a nursing home."

Nothing Sam said could dissuade her, so he stopped arguing. It was her life, after all. And maybe the exercise would do her good. He'd read about an eighty-one-year-old man who had hiked the entire length of the Appalachian Trail, 2,168 miles. What were old people thinking these days? In comparison, he supposed pedaling her bicycle around Hope wouldn't kill his mother.

"It is a pretty bike," he conceded. "Has Dad seen it yet?"

"No, I didn't even tell him I was buying one. You know how your father is. He would have told me not to waste the money. He would have gone to the landfill and found bike parts and cobbled one together for me."

"Well, you're right there," Sam said.

"Besides, I've never had a brand-new bicycle. All the bikes I've had were hand-me-downs," she said. "Take it for a spin, see what you think."

Sam took several turns around the meetinghouse parking lot. It beat any bike he'd ever had, that was for sure.

"What you ought to do," he said, coasting to a stop, "is buy some baskets for it so you can ride it to the grocery store."

"Now you're talking."

They went inside and phoned Charley Riggle, who checked his catalog and determined that baskets could indeed be purchased and ordered a pair of them.

"Riding my bike to the store," Sam's mother said, clapping her hands. "Just like when I was a little girl."

She stayed for lunch, then left for home, while Sam visited the sick and shut-ins. The meeting was mercifully short on shut-ins, but Dan Woodrum was having a heart catheterization the next day, so Sam went to wish him well and pray for him, which Dan seemed to appreciate.

"Are you worried?" Sam asked.

"Not too much. Pretty routine procedure for men my age."

"I hope you don't need a bypass."

"Me, too."

They talked for a while about people they'd known whose hearts had exploded, each one trying to top the other with a more gruesome story until Dan Woodrum was so thoroughly terrified he wished Sam hadn't bothered to visit.

"I had this one guy in my first church," Sam said, while taking his leave, "whose chest wall was literally ripped apart by a heart attack. Might as well have been hit by a Mack truck. But don't you worry, you're going to be fine."

Then he hugged Dan and left, pleased to have been of help.

The talk of mortality made him uneasy. He hadn't exercised in months. Maybe he could mow the yard. It was probably too early, except here and there were clumps of wild onions and high tufts of green grass. Maybe he could knock the top off, as his father said. He filled the mower with gas, checked the oil, cleaned the spark plug, then pushed the mower from the garage to the driveway. It started on the fifth pull, beginning with a barking sputter before catching hold.

He mowed back and forth in neat lines, enjoying the feeling of accomplishment. Lawn mowing provided immediate gratification, which he liked. Everything else he did took time to show results, if it ever did. His mind drifted to the building addition, wondering whether it would actually happen. Quakers were notoriously slow about such matters.

Lost in thought, he didn't notice the nest of bunnies in a hump of grass, so didn't stop the mower in time. Horrified, he shut off the mower, looking around to make sure no one had seen him annihilate an entire rabbit family. Thank God that Barbara was still at school. He couldn't even tell how many he had killed. He thought of counting the legs and dividing by four, but couldn't bring himself to look at them. He hurried inside and retrieved an old Tupperware container Barbara wouldn't miss, then pulled on a pair of work gloves and began picking up the mangled carcasses as quickly as he could.

This was the worst thing he'd ever done. He'd go down in the annals of rabbitdom as a serial killer. The good feeling he'd had from ministering to Dan Woodrum was gone. He couldn't throw the dead rabbits away. Barbara would find them. She had a nose for things like that. He decided to bury them and found a place in the backyard, where she seldom ventured, behind a redbud tree. The rabbits would like it there, he thought. He dug down two feet, placed the Tupperware container in the grave, said a brief prayer for the rabbits, thanking God for letting him know the rabbits, and now entrusting them back to His care. He hadn't actually known the rabbits, and the rabbits were probably wishing their paths had never crossed, but it somehow seemed fitting to pray such a prayer at a rabbit funeral. He filled the hole with dirt, rounding it off in a neat little mound, then returned the shovel to the garage.

He was finishing the yard when Barbara pulled in the driveway. He had thought he might tell her about the rabbits, but decided against it. No woman wanted to be married to a man capable of such cruelty, even if the cruelty was a result of negligence. Some stories were better left untold. So he told her about Dan Woodrum instead, and how he had been such a comfort to him.

"You have such a good heart," Barbara told him, which felt good to hear, even though Sam had his doubts.

17

I saw our old pastor at the grocery store today," Stacey
Maxwell told her husband, Herb, at supper that evening.
"Did he ask where we'd been?"
"Yes."
"What did you tell him?" Herb asked.
"I told him we were attending a Quaker meeting and I told
him why, that we didn't like being harangued about money."
Herb chuckled. "What did he have to say about that?"
"Personally, he seemed glad to be rid of us. I think he likes
his followers to be more docile."
After dinner, Herb washed the dishes and picked up the living
room while Stacey readied the twins for bed, then they
collapsed on the couch.
"So are we going to become Quakers or not?" Herb asked.
"I don't see anyone pressuring us to join. Let's not jump
into it like we did the last church."
"I agree," Herb said. "I want to get to know them better before
joining. For all we know, they could be snake-handlers."
Stacey had been on the Internet, reading about Quakers, and
to her great relief hadn't come across anything about snakes.

That would have been a tough one to explain to her parents, raising their grandchildren in a church full of rattlesnakes.

"So what did you do today?" Stacey asked.

"Led a workshop on nutrition for the players. You wouldn't believe what those guys eat in the off-season. I'm surprised they're not all dead."

"No cheerleader physicals, eh?"

"Nope, not today. How about you? What did you do?" Herb asked.

"Changed diapers, kept the kids fed, went to the grocery store, and cleaned the house," Stacey said.

It wasn't quite the life she had imagined while in law school. No better, no worse, just different. Just life.

"You're exhausted, honey. Why don't you go to bed, and I'll pick up the house and get the laundry going," Herb said.

It was his favorite part of the day, mindless activity at the end of the day, his wife and children asleep. Standing over the babies while they slept, watching their bodies rise and fall with each breath.

He hadn't counted on any of this—his family, his house, his job. His parents had divorced when he was young, he'd been raised by his mother, perpetually poor, but had landed a college scholarship, met and married Stacey, borrowed money for his medical school and her law school, graduated, the twins were born, and here they were, a family.

His father had died ten years before; his mother had remarried and moved south. No aunts, no uncles, just his wife and the twins, and maybe a new church and the potential for friends. He hoped so anyway. He washed the dishes and put them in the drainer to dry, folded the first load of laundry, then went to bed, settling into the curve of his wife's back, deeply happy.

18

Charles Gardner had spent the past three weeks studying the floors in their home, hoping if he contemplated them long enough, someone might come along and volunteer to sand them. Ideally, one of his sons, who seemed impervious to his hints.

"They have their own lives, and they both work," Gloria said. "You can't expect them to give up vacation days to work on our house. You're retired. You do it."

And he would have done it, except he feared if he were competent he would be expected to make more repairs. He was starting to wish they'd moved into a condo. What had he been thinking, moving into this old wreck of a house? Gloria had warned against it, but he hadn't listened. Now it was too late.

On top of that, he feared his wife might be losing her mind. Buying a bicycle? What had she been thinking? She was going to end up dead, smashed by a car, her head caved in, flatter than a fritter. She had told him not to worry. Easy enough for her to say. Who would cook for him with her gone? He'd raised the subject with Sam, who'd dismissed his concerns and then changed the subject altogether.

"Say, Dad, you ought to get a heart scan. Dan Woodrum just had a heart cath and they found a blockage. You have the same symptoms he had. Your color isn't good. You're tired all the time."

"I'm tired all the time because no one will help me with this house. Maybe if I had help, I wouldn't be so tired."

"Dad, you might have to hire someone to help you, like everyone else. I work full-time, and so does Roger."

"I tried telling him that," Gloria Gardner said. "But he doesn't listen to me."

Charles and Gloria began bickering, so Sam slipped out in mid-argument and headed toward home, stopping to see Dan Woodrum, who was recovering at home from his heart procedure. He was sitting in a recliner, watching the National Geographic channel. He waved Sam into the house.

"Come in, come in. Thanks for coming to see me."

"How are you feeling, Dan?"

"Great. Everything went well. Slid a balloon into my left anterior descending artery and opened it right up. I feel great."

"Ah, the ol' left anterior descending artery," Sam said. "They can sure be troublesome."

Sam stayed a half hour, marveling at medical science and Dan's quick recovery, then walked home, feeling a twinge in his chest every now and then, fretting about his left anterior descending artery and how long he might have to live.

19

It had been a good many years since Hank Withers applied for a building permit of any sort, and he was amazed at how complicated the process had become. Meetings to attend, fees to pay, stacks of paperwork to fill out, signatures to gather, securing the approval of neighbors, sucking up to plan commissions and zoning boards; there was no end to it. A lady from the county environmental board showed up late one afternoon and spent three hours studying the earth to be moved, in search of rare flowers and insects, making sure they weren't building on top of an Indian burial ground.

"When I started in this business fifty years ago," Hank told the lady, "you could pretty much build wherever you wanted, so long as it wasn't in a flood plain."

"It's certainly gotten more complicated," the lady agreed.

Hank regaled her with stories of the good old days before all the rules and regulations, which had caused nothing but trouble as far as he was concerned.

"There hasn't been an Indian on this land in two hundred years," he complained.

It was nearing dusk. She was studying a hickory tree, peering into the upper reaches with a pair of binoculars. "Did you realize there's a nesting colony of Indiana bats in this tree?" she asked him.

"Yeah, they get into the meetinghouse every now and then," Hank said. "We have to swat them with a tennis racket."

"You kill them?"

"It's no big deal. There's more where they came from," Hank said.

"I beg your pardon. It's a very big deal. Indiana bats fall under the protection of the Endangered Species Act."

"We really don't kill them," Hank said, backpedaling. "We just open the windows and use the tennis racket to guide them outside. We wouldn't think of hurting one." Hank hated bats, and the previous summer had personally ushered a dozen or so of them to their eternal rest.

"We can't grant a building permit until this colony leaves the tree and enters hibernation," the lady said. "Even then you won't be able to cut down these trees. They're a bat habitat."

"But that tree's gotta go," Hank argued. "It's right where our new kitchen is going to be."

"I'm sorry, but the bats are a protected species."

"That's the dumbest thing I've ever heard. They're all over the place around here in the summer. Hundreds of them, maybe thousands. They boil out of these trees at night."

The lady seemed pleased by that news and phoned her boss to report that a thriving colony of Indiana bats had been discovered.

The next day, early in the morning, a half-dozen officers from the Department of Natural Resources swarmed the meetinghouse grounds, climbed the trees, inspected the meetinghouse attic, collected bat poop in plastic bags, then presented Sam with an order demanding Hope Friends Meeting not only halt all efforts to build but also not enter the meetinghouse, which had a colony of Indiana bats in the attic, mating frantically, and were not to be disturbed under any circumstances.

"I don't want anyone near this meetinghouse," the man in charge said, who had a hairy, scrunched face and looked something like a bat himself. "Bats stress very easily and it will ruin their reproductive cycle."

"We can't go in our own meetinghouse?" Sam asked, incredulous. "Where will we meet?"

"Not my problem," said the bat man.

"How long do we have to stay out?"

"Three months, maybe four."

"Can I at least get my computer?" Sam asked.

"Yes, but hurry."

Sam retrieved his computer, carried it across the parking lot to the parsonage, then phoned Ruby Hopper to report that bats had taken up residence in the meetinghouse attic, were engaged in loose and reckless sex, and the state had sided with the bats.

"Well," Ruby said, "we're always talking about caring for the environment. I suppose we can give up our meetinghouse for three months if it means helping God's creation."

"That's not all," Sam added. "We can't build until the bats migrate for hibernation, and even then we can't cut down trees to build onto our meetinghouse."

Sam was warming to the idea of closing the meetinghouse, thinking he might parlay it into a three-month paid vacation, which would allow him and Barbara to drive west to the redwoods, or maybe head east to Bradford, Pennsylvania, and tour the Case pocketknife factory and museum. Maybe even work in a visit to Georgia, where their son Addison was stationed. He was beginning to feel kindly toward the bats.

"I guess I better start calling folks to let them know meeting for worship is canceled for the next three months," he said.

"Let's hold off on that," Ruby suggested. "I see no reason to cancel meeting for worship. We can certainly find somewhere else to meet. Let's not tell the rest of the meeting until we have a plan of action."

And just that quickly, Sam's dream of a summer off faded and was gone.

At the precise moment Sam was watching his summer vacation vanish into thin air, his mother crossed an intersection on her bicycle and was clobbered by a car driven by a teenage girl who was texting and blew through a stop sign, crashing into the rear tire of Gloria's bicycle, causing her to sail through the air and land on the opposite sidewalk in a battered heap. She had always dreaded the thought of languishing in a nursing home, so wasn't altogether displeased at the prospect of dying quickly in an accident. She lay quietly on the sidewalk, gathering her thoughts, taking a mental inventory of any possible broken bones, moving her limbs one at a time. In the distance, she heard a siren and a young girl screaming, and the siren and screams became one, and then she heard nothing.

20

A memory. Sam was in eighth grade, acutely aware of girls, most of whom seemed acutely unaware of him. So when Uly Grant, his best friend, told him Kathy Thompson hoped Sam would invite her to the eighth-grade dance, he didn't believe him. The next week, Kathy, in clear violation of the accepted protocol, asked him to the dance, and Sam was so shocked he said yes, before it occurred to him he had never danced, except when he was home and pretended he was on *American Bandstand* and Dick Clark himself had singled him out as a fine example of rhythm.

Rhythm had never been Sam's strong suit, and he had thought of calling Kathy the morning of the dance and telling her he was deathly ill with the bubonic plague, but his mother wouldn't let him. Instead, she put on their Andy Williams albums and spent the afternoon teaching him how to dance. After three hours of practice, he still wasn't very good, but was good enough for an eighth-grade dance. Good enough not to embarrass himself.

The evening had gone about like he'd thought it would.

Kathy spent most of the night in the girls' restroom with her friends. Sam and Uly had stood by the punch bowl, eating cookies baked by Mrs. Selser's home-ec class. Sam and Kathy had danced twice, both fast dances. The last dance was a slow dance, when they were supposed to dance while holding one another, but by then Sam was sick from the punch and cookies and had excused himself to go outside and barf. Uly had taken Kathy home, and they fell in love and dated the entire summer before high school, which had upset Sam at first until he realized that love and romance had made Uly miserable, then he was grateful Uly had spared him that particular misery.

The week of the dance, Sam's mother had driven him to Crowley's Menswear in Cartersburg and bought him a new suit with money she'd saved for a new Easter outfit for herself, which he didn't realize at the time, and found out only when he overheard his father criticize her for wasting their money on a suit that would be worn only once before Sam grew out of it.

"It's my money. I earned it, and if I want to spend it on Sam, I will," she'd told him.

It was late at night. His parents were sitting in the kitchen next to the cold air return, so Sam heard every word through the heating duct in his bedroom. He'd been listening to their private conversations for years, something he usually enjoyed, though he felt odd hearing this one.

His dad had been tight with money. His mom made her money working for Johnny Mackey, cleaning the funeral home. Two dollars an hour. His new suit had cost eighty dollars. Forty hours of emptying ashtrays, vacuuming carpets, cleaning toilets, and digging out snotty Kleenexes from the sofa cushions. He'd vowed then and there to make it up to her.

Maybe buy her a new refrigerator or stove when he got his first job. Then he got his first job and bought himself a car instead. Then the kids came, and there was never extra money after that.

He'd brought it up in conversation once, when his kids were little. They were talking about the things parents did for their children, and Sam said he'd heard about this mother who'd worked forty hours to buy her son a suit for his eighth-grade dance, and she'd gotten embarrassed and told him to pipe down.

He'd never gotten around to getting her a new refrigerator. Now she was pushing eighty and probably on her last refrigerator. Maybe he could get her a stove instead. Or a water softener. Or maybe a vacuum cleaner he'd seen advertised on TV that had enough suction to pick up a bowling ball, though not many people had bowling balls lying around on their floors. But something like that, something that said he cared.

21

The EMTs found Gloria Gardner on the sidewalk, dazed, babbling incoherently, clammy and shocky, unable to pronounce her name. They searched her pockets and found Barbara Gardner's name and cell phone number on a scrap of paper with a note to phone her about the new meetinghouse kitchen and whether it should have two sinks or three. They phoned Barbara to tell her an elderly woman, with Barbara's name in her pocket, had been struck by a car while riding a bicycle and was on her way to the hospital.

A bicycle? Who did she know who was elderly and rode a bicycle? Then Barbara remembered Charles Gardner grumbling something about Gloria riding a bicycle. She phoned Sam, but he was talking to Wilson Roberts to tell him they'd been evicted from their meetinghouse by fornicating bats, so she called her father-in-law, Charles Gardner, who wasn't wearing his hearing aids and thought she was a telemarketer so hung up the phone.

Barbara found Sam at home, still gabbing away, pried the

phone from his hand, loaded him in the car, and headed toward the hospital.

"Is she dead?" Sam asked. "Tell me what they told you."

"Just that she's been in an accident. We don't know if she's alive or dead. They didn't tell me. They just told us to get to the hospital."

"I better call Roger and Dad. And Levi and Addison, too."

"Not yet. Let's wait until we know something. No sense in worrying everyone."

Gloria Gardner was sitting up in bed, in the emergency room, by the time Sam and Barbara tracked her down. A nurse was bandaging her knees, which were scraped raw, while Gloria was ranting about young people and the dangers of texting.

"She didn't even slow down for the stop sign. Just plowed right into me. I'm lucky I'm not dead."

"You're lucky you didn't land on your head and bash your brains out," Sam said, finding his voice after his initial shock had worn off. "I thought I told you to wear a helmet."

The doctor strolled into the room, carrying X-rays, which he clipped on the view box.

"No fractures," he said, studying the screen. "You were incredibly lucky, Mrs. Gardner. But if I were you, I'd give up bicycling."

"Absolutely not, it's the one thing I enjoy."

"Then please wear a helmet and be more careful," the doctor said. "Watch out for cars. You're going to lose every time you go up against one."

"She's the one who ran the stop sign," Gloria snapped. "Not me."

"If you're dead, it doesn't really matter whose fault it was, now does it," the doctor pointed out. "If you're going to ride,

ride defensively. Assume cars don't see you, and for God's sake, get a helmet."

"How long do I have to stay here?"

"You're free to leave. You're going to be really sore, so I'm giving you a prescription for pain medicine. Go easy on it, though, it's powerful stuff. Get back here immediately if you notice blood in your stool."

The doctor studied her pupils once more, asked a few questions, then departed.

Sam, Barbara, and Gloria waited in the room.

"I didn't care for his attitude," Gloria said.

"He's probably tired of seeing people die from preventable accidents," Sam pointed out.

"Oh, before I forget, Barbara. They put me on the kitchen committee of the new meetinghouse addition. I've been thinking about sinks. Do you think we should put in two sinks or three?"

"Do we have to talk about this now?" Sam said.

"We might as well talk about it now, while we're waiting," Gloria said.

"I'd go with three," Barbara said. "I've never wished there were fewer sinks."

Barbara and Gloria moved on to the topic of stoves, then, mercifully, a nurse entered the room, pushing a wheelchair. She helped Gloria off the bed and eased her into the chair. Gloria signed the papers authorizing the hospital to share her information with the insurance company and the government and anyone else who might have a stake in the matter, then the nurse wheeled Gloria out of the emergency room to the outside door, and waited while Sam pulled up the car.

"Where's my bike?" she asked Sam, once she was settled in the backseat.

"I have no idea, and right now I'm not inclined to find out."

He'd forgotten all about her picking up snotty Kleenex for forty hours to buy him a suit.

They stopped at the pharmacy on the way home, bought her pain medicine, then helped her up the stairs of her house and onto her front porch, where they deposited her in a rocking chair. They found Sam's father on the couch, napping. He'd been doing a lot of that lately, as if the thought of all the work the house needed wore him out. Sam shook him awake.

"Mom got hit by a car and darn near died," he told his father. "She's out on the front porch. You might want to go be with her."

Charles Gardner raised himself off the couch, panicked. "What do you mean she darn near died? What's wrong with her?"

"She was riding her bicycle and got hit by a car, that's what wrong with her. But she's okay, just banged up a little."

"Why didn't someone call me?"

"Barbara tried, Dad. But you weren't wearing your hearing aids, and you hung up on her."

"Those things drive me crazy. Always whistling and buzzing. I told you I didn't want them."

It was in that moment, Sam Gardner had a glimpse of his future. Two parents in generally good health, but stubborn and uncooperative. And they could last for years. Decades, maybe. He needed a nap just thinking about it.

22

Sam and Barbara stayed an hour or so, making sure his mother was all right, then left before Sam was roped into sanding floors.

"Are you going back to work?" Sam asked Barbara as they pulled away from the curb.

"No, I'm not, and neither are you. You're taking me to Bruno's and I'm going to have a big plate of lasagna and a glass of wine, and if anyone comes in and tells me a minister's wife shouldn't drink wine, I'm going to beat them over the head until they're dead."

So they went to Bruno's, where Bruno himself welcomed them warmly, fussed over Barbara, and escorted them to a corner table.

Bruno poured Barbara a glass of wine, then invited himself to sit with them.

"You look discouraged," he said to Sam. "What's wrong?"

"Just worn out," Sam said. "My mom is riding a bicycle around town—flirting with death. And our meetinghouse is full of bats and we can't meet there for three, maybe four, months."

"Bats? What kind of bats?"

"Indiana bats. They're protected by the government and are, even as we speak, reproducing like rabbits in our meetinghouse attic. So we can't go in there for three months. Maybe four."

"Aw, romance," Bruno said. "It's just like Cole Porter said. The birds do it, the bees do it, even educated fleas do it."

"And now the bats are doing it and we don't have a place to meet," Sam grumbled.

"Meet outside, under the trees," Bruno suggested.

"They're doing it in the trees, too," Sam said.

"You should ask the priest at Our Lady of Hope if you can use our fellowship hall," Bruno said. "It sits empty on Sunday afternoons."

"That's a thought," said Sam. "What would you charge?"

"Probably nothing, since you're a church," Bruno said. "What's your cell phone number? I'll send you our priest's telephone number."

Sam recited his number, which Bruno punched into his own phone, then sent Sam the priest's information.

Bruno excused himself to fix their lasagna, then returned with a bottle of wine, topping off Barbara's glass. Sam took a sip. He didn't ordinarily care for alcohol, but the wine was surprisingly pleasant, so he asked for a glass. "Just a little," he told Bruno. "I'm not used to this stuff."

The lasagna came, and Bruno left the bottle of wine on their table.

"Here, have a little more," Barbara said. "'A little wine for thy stomach's sake,' First Timothy, chapter five, verse twenty-three."

"Maybe just a little more," Sam agreed. "I wouldn't want to disobey the Bible."

It had been a rough day, what with frisky bats and his mother getting hit by a car and his father bellyaching about his hearing aids and having to find a new place for Hope Friends to meet, but somehow the wine made him forget all his problems after a while.

"Say, this is pretty tasty," he told Bruno, pouring himself a third glass. "What do they call this?"

"It's my house wine."

"Nice and nutty," Sam said, who didn't know the first thing about wine. He drank his third glass in one fell swoop, then leaned back, his eyes glazed over, smiling contentedly, draped like a wet noodle in his chair.

Barbara had known Sam over thirty years, and in all that time had never seen him finish a glass of wine. But now, from what she could tell, he was three sheets to the wind, going on four. She eased the empty glass from his hand and handed it to Bruno.

"What do you put in that house wine of yours, anyway?" she asked Bruno.

"Nothing but grapes."

"Those must be powerful grapes," Barbara said. "He's plastered."

Sam leaned over toward Barbara and kissed her check. "Isn't she the most beautiful woman you've ever seen?" he said to no one in particular. "Thirty years we've been married and she's still a wildcat, if you know what I mean."

"Be quiet, Sam," Barbara said.

"Why don't you give me a kiss, little wildcat?" He said it loudly. There were a dozen other people in the restaurant, all of whom turned to stare at Sam.

"She can still fit in her wedding dress," Sam announced to

the room. "Hasn't gained a pound in all the years we've been married. Sure, she's a little broad across the beam, but that's to be expected when you get to be her age."

"Pipe down, Sam," Barbara hissed. "Bruno, help me get him to the car, please."

They lifted Sam to his feet and headed toward the door. Sam began to sing, loudly, "The birds do it, the bees do it, even educated fleas do it. Let's do it. Let's fall in love."

He turned to Barbara. "Do you love me?"

"Yes, I love you, but now we have to go home, so let's go. You're going to have to help us, Sam. Try to walk."

"I love you, honey." He turned to face the other patrons. "Her ankles have gotten a little thicker since we got married, but that's all. Well, that and her bottom, but nothing else. She's the best wife ever."

"Let's go, Sam," Bruno said, hurrying him along.

"We've got to call that priest and see about using the church. I'll just tell him I have bats in my attic. I bet he'll help me. I'd help him, after all," Sam said, much too loudly. "One minister helping another, just like the good Lord told us to do."

And on that ecumenical note, Sam collapsed, done in by three glasses of wine.

23

⌣

I knew it would come to this," Gloria Gardner wailed. "He'd move to the city and fall in with the wrong crowd and start drinking."

Barbara had enlisted the help of her mother-in-law, who, despite her own infirmities, was helping Sam into his house.

"I can't believe three glasses of wine did this," Barbara said.

They helped him up the stairs and onto the front porch and through the door to the living room couch, where they stretched him out.

"It's his father's fault," Gloria said. "His grandfather was a terrible drunk. It looks like Sam got the gene. My son, an alcoholic." She teared up thinking about it.

"I don't think getting drunk one time in fifty-four years makes him an alcoholic," Barbara said. "He just has a low tolerance for alcohol, that's all."

"And is Charles Gardner here to help his son? Not on your life. He's probably off sitting in some bar getting plastered."

In the thirty-plus years Barbara had known Charles Gardner, he'd never drank anything stronger than prune juice, but now Gloria had him passed out on Skid Row.

Sam stirred on the couch, moaning and clutching his head. "I think I'm going to be sick," he groaned, then promptly vomited.

"Lying there in the gutter, wasting his life," Gloria Gardner wailed.

"He's not lying in the gutter and he's not wasting his life. He's just not used to alcohol. He'll be fine once he sleeps it off."

As if commanded, Sam fell back on the couch and began to snore.

"Some husband and father he turned out to be," Gloria said.

"You're not helping. Now let's get this mess cleaned up."

"You do that," she said, leaving the room. "I'm going to search the garage and make sure he's not hiding booze somewhere. I bet he's got it stashed all over the place."

There was a knock on the door. "Is anybody home?"

It was Leonard and Wanda Fink, letting themselves in. They stared at Sam, then noticed the vomit.

"You might want to stay back, I think he has the flu," Barbara said, ushering the Finks toward the door.

Leonard Fink sniffed the air disapprovingly. "We just came by to clean the meetinghouse. We're going to wash windows. Do you have some paper towels we can use?"

"Yes, yes, just don't come in. I don't want you to get sick, too." Barbara hurried to the pantry, retrieved two rolls of paper towels, and gave them to Leonard. "Now if you'll excuse me, I have to tend to Sam."

The Finks departed, and Barbara helped Sam into the bathroom, stripped off his clothes, put him in the shower, and tossed his clothes in the washer.

Sam stood in the shower until the hot water ran out, then endured the cold water as long as he could, until his mind cleared and the throbbing in his head subsided. He toweled off, then shaved and combed his hair for the second time that day, pulled on clean clothes, all the while vowing never to drink again.

He hoped he hadn't said or done anything embarrassing while he'd been drunk. Something that would come back to haunt him. He remembered Barbara urging him not to be so loud at Bruno's, but that's all he remembered. He remembered Bruno telling him to call the priest at Our Lady of Hope, and remembered eating lasagna and drinking the first glass of wine. After that, everything was a blur. He hoped he hadn't said anything about Gretchen Weber, Ruby Hopper's niece, who he was secretly infatuated with because of her French braid. No, he couldn't have said anything about her since he was still alive and Barbara seemed cheerful enough. He could hear her humming in the kitchen. That was a good sign.

His mother came in the back door. "Well, I tore the garage apart, but couldn't find any booze. Sam must have drunk it all."

"Of course, another option exists," Barbara said. "Maybe you didn't find any because there wasn't any to find."

Sam walked into the kitchen, slowly, carefully. "Mom, I've never drank that much. That was the first time ever, I promise. And it'll be the last time."

"Your great-grandfather on your father's side was an alcoholic, you know. It skips a generation, then comes back."

"Then that would make Dad an alcoholic, not me," Sam pointed out.

Gloria Gardner was in no mood for reason, and told him she didn't see how she could leave him any inheritance knowing he would drink it all away.

"I'm sure glad you weren't hurt today," Sam said, changing the subject.

"It could have been a lot worse," she admitted. "I suppose I'll have to get a new bike now that mine is ruined."

"Or maybe this experience could help you realize it's not safe for someone your age to be riding a bicycle," Sam said.

"Nonsense! I was doing just fine until that young lady ran the stop sign. That had nothing to do with my age."

Sam sighed. Between the bats, his mother, and the Finks, Sam thought maybe he'd keep drinking after all.

24

eonard and Wanda Fink were washing the meetinghouse windows, working their way around the inside of the meetinghouse, when Wanda pulled back a curtain and a bat flew out and hit her smack in the face, causing her to fall off the stepladder and land on Leonard, who fell backward and landed on the floor with his wife on top of him. It was the most intimate contact they'd had in years, and they found it most unpleasant.

The bat circled the inside of the meetinghouse, dipping and diving. Wanda army-crawled over to a table and hid underneath it, while Leonard tore after the bat, swinging at it, trying to knock it to the floor. It skimmed over his head, back and forth across the room, then flew up to the ceiling and disappeared into a slight crack between the drywall and a beam.

"Oh, my Lord, there must have been a dozen of them," Wanda said. "What were they?"

"Bats! And where there's one, there's a hundred."

Leonard hurried outside to the utility shed and retrieved a ladder, which he used to shinny up through the access door

into the meetinghouse attic. He flipped on the light switch, il-
luminating the darkened attic, causing scores of bats to take
flight, looping and swirling and bobbing in the hot, stale air.
Ordinarily, he would have called for a meeting of the trustees,
perhaps found some pertinent Scripture on the eradication of
bats, prayed about it at length, for a year or two or possibly
three. But this was no time for deliberation. He returned to
the shed and found a two-by-four, the length of a baseball
bat, which when grasped with both hands and swung made a
formidable weapon. He hustled back inside, scurried up the
ladder—it was the fastest he'd moved in years—and began
swatting at the bats, charging through the attic in a mad frenzy,
killing the bats in droves as they hung on the rafters, until their
dying, twitching bodies littered the attic floor.

"What are you doing up there?" Wanda yelled.

"Getting rid of these bats. You wouldn't believe it up here.
There's bat poop everywhere. Go get me a shovel out of the
shed and hand me up some trash bags."

He gathered the dead bats into one bag, then scooped the
guano into another bag, doing a thorough job of it, removing
every trace of the bats. In the meetingroom, Wanda finished
washing the windows, carefully pulling aside the curtains,
ready to dive to the floor if necessary.

She was cleaning the last window when Leonard climbed
down the ladder, his grisly work completed.

"There must be a dozen places where I can see daylight
coming in through openings," he told Wanda. "I'm going to
Riggle's Hardware to get some caulk and close up those holes.
I'll be right back."

He drove to the hardware store, chatted with Charley, the
owner, about their bat infestation, then returned to the meet-

inghouse, climbed back into the attic, and caulked every opening shut until no daylight shone through anywhere, sealing out the bats. Then he worked his way through the attic, shining his flashlight, doing one last sweep for bats. He found three more clinging upside down to a rafter, and swiftly, gleefully, dispatched them to bat hell.

He lowered the trash bags to Wanda, then climbed back down the ladder, shutting the attic door behind him. "We've just saved the meeting a thousand dollars," he bragged to Wanda. "They would have called some pest control company who would have charged good money to do what I just did for a hundred dollars a week."

"And they got their windows washed to boot," Wanda said.

"Maybe now Sam will see the wisdom in hiring us," Leonard said. "He was against it, you know."

Wanda snorted in disgust.

They carried the trash bags out to their car, depositing them in the trunk. "The guano we'll take home for the garden. The bats we'll set out at the end of the driveway. Tomorrow's trash day."

"You know," Wanda said after they had deposited the bag of bats at the meetinghouse curb, "if everyone in this meeting worked as hard as we did, there'd be more people here and we could hire us a decent pastor."

"You got that right," Leonard said.

They drove home in blissful ignorance, having cheerfully obliterated one of the remaining colonies of the rapidly declining Indiana bat, who, though considerably smaller than Leonard and Wanda Fink, did considerably more good.

25

Herb and Stacey Maxwell's poodle, Precious, was the first to sniff out the bag of bats, after he slipped out their back door when Herb went outside to roll their trash container down to the curb. Precious cut across the neighbor's yard, rounded their house with Herb in hot pursuit, then made a beeline for the meetinghouse woods, which is where Herb lost him.

Precious was a spiteful little dog, an animal that gave the otherwise virtuous species a bad name. He had belonged to Stacey's spinster aunt, who had died the year before, but not before making Stacey promise to care for Precious until he died. He was only two years old, committing them to a decade of indentured servitude. Herb would have happily knocked off Precious and tossed him in the aunt's casket, but Stacey wouldn't hear of it. Her aunt had set up a trust fund for Precious, twenty thousand dollars, to provide for his care and finance his funeral. The dog ate better than they did.

Herb walked slowly through the trees, pausing now and

then to listen for Precious, before realizing that Precious running away was an unanticipated blessing, so he quit while he was ahead, returned home, hauled the trash to the curb, and went inside to report that Precious had run away.

"What do you mean, he ran away?" Stacey asked, alarmed. She didn't like Precious, either, but felt a deeper obligation than Herb, having promised her dying aunt she'd look after him. "We can't just let him go. You watch the kids, and I'll go look for Precious." She snagged the dog's leash on her way out the door.

She found Precious at the end of the meetinghouse lane, tearing into the trash bag, a bat clamped in his mouth, shaking it to ensure its death, then proceeding to eat it, leathery wings and all.

Stacey clipped the leash onto Precious's collar, then nudged the bag open with her foot, recoiling in disgust when the bats fell out on the ground. How disgusting! What were the Gardners doing with a bag of dead bats? She didn't know much about Quakerism, but was reasonably certain it didn't involve animal sacrifice.

She pulled Precious away from the bag, then reached down to wrest the bat away from the loathsome little poodle and was bitten soundly on the hand. Precious clamped down, piercing Stacey's skin, digging into tendon and muscle, rupturing capillaries, grazing bone. The dog hung on, snarling, grinding down harder on Stacey's hand, until in desperation she drew back her foot and shoved him squarely on the rump, forcing him to let go.

She stumbled home, pulling Precious behind her, who continued to snarl and snap at her, baring his evil fangs. Lord, she hated that dog. She began calling out for Herb as soon as she entered their yard. He hurried out their front door, a crying baby in each arm. If her hand hadn't hurt so much, she'd have laughed at the absurdity of their situation. With commendable agility, Herb took the leash in one hand, and placed a baby in her good arm.

He deposited the dog in the garage, hoping it would lick up antifreeze and die, then hurried to collect the other baby from Stacey, who was now turning pale from shock. He carried the twins into the house and placed them in their cribs, grabbed a roll of paper towels, and hurried outside to help Stacey into the kitchen, where he sat her on a stool in front of the sink and ran cool water over her hand, wincing as the blood swirled away to expose white bone.

Although he was a doctor, he had never cared for the sight of blood, and felt woozy, but collected himself, and dialed 911.

"I'm getting an ambulance here. We need to get you to the emergency room," he told Stacey with a calmness he didn't feel.

He gave their address to the dispatcher, described the problem, then hung up the phone and turned back to Stacey.

"We need someone to come watch the babies. I'm going to call the Gardners. Sam gave me his cell number this past Sunday."

He began scrolling through his contacts, looking for the Gs.

"No, not them," Stacey said.

"Why not? They said to call them if we ever needed help."

"I don't trust them."

"What do you mean, you don't trust them? He's a Quaker minister and she's an elementary school librarian. What's not to trust?"

"I found a bag of dead bats at their curb," Stacey said. "Precious was eating one and he bit me when I took it away from him. I think they're involved in animal sacrifice, possibly Satan worship."

"A bag of dead bats? Are you sure? People just don't have bags of dead bats. Are you sure that's what they were?"

"Yes, I'm sure. I know what a bat looks like."

"And Precious was eating one and then he bit you?"

"Yes."

In the distance, he could hear the ambulance siren. "Stay here. Don't move. Don't touch the babies."

He ran to his car, opened the trunk, rummaged around, and found a box of latex gloves. He pulled one on each hand, ran back in the house for a sandwich bag, then hurried to the Gardners' curb, where he did indeed find a garbage bag full of dead bats, one of them partially consumed.

"I'll be darned, it is a bat," he muttered. He picked up the chewed-on bat and placed it in the sandwich bag, pressed the two sides together until the bag sealed, then shoved it in his pocket.

The ambulance pulled up in their driveway and Herb showed the EMTs into their house, introduced himself, then described his wife's injuries.

"I want her taken to the university hospital. When we get there, I want someone to meet us from the lab who can run a rabies test on a dead bat."

"Your wife was attacked by a bat?" one of the EMTs asked.

"No, she was bit by a dog who had just consumed part of a bat. I want to make sure the bat wasn't rabid."

"Where's the dog?"

"In our garage," Herb said. "It's not going anywhere."

Ezra and Emma were still howling.

"I'm going to get my children and meet you at the hospital," he said.

He threw a half-dozen diapers and two bottles into their diaper bag, carried the twins outside, and secured them in their baby seats. The ride to the hospital quieted them, giving him time to think. The Gardners were Satan worshippers? He didn't believe it. Then again, it was an odd world, and he had heard of stranger things.

26

Sam's reputation was taking a thrashing.

"Did you know your son had an alcohol problem?" Gloria Gardner said to her husband.

"Oh, don't be silly. Sam doesn't drink. He hates alcohol."

"No, he *hated* alcohol. Past tense. But now it appears he's developed a fondness for it. He got drunk today at Bruno's."

"Did you hit your head when that car hit you? You seem a little off," Charles Gardner said.

"No, I did not hit my head. And I know what I saw. Barbara and I practically had to pour him onto the couch."

"Well, I'll be. I never would have figured Sam for that. Roger, maybe, but never Sam."

Gloria began to weep. She had worked so hard to shepherd her sons through the perils of life, and was so proud of both of them. Now, just when she had begun to relax, had begun to breathe easy, Sam had spiraled out of control.

"Maybe we ought to do one of those interference things that they do with alcoholics," Charles Gardner suggested.

"What's that?"

"It's something I saw on television once. You get all the family together, and some friends and maybe people from the church, and you set the alcoholic down and interfere with him."

"How do you interfere with him?"

"Well, you try to make him see that he's hurt people, and try to make him cry, and admit that he's got a problem."

They sat quietly, contemplating the sad twist their lives had taken.

"We need to call Ruby Hopper and let her know what's going on," Gloria Gardner said. "After all, she's the clerk of the meeting."

"I suppose you're right."

They phoned Ruby to report the bitter news. Ruby was shocked, and said she'd not seen the first indication that Sam had a drinking problem. "I've not smelled it on him. Barbara's not said a thing to me."

"His great-grandfather was a boozehound," Gloria Gardner reported solemnly. "It's in his genes."

"I just can't believe it," Ruby said. "Sam is the last person I would ever have suspected of that."

"Believe me, we're shocked, too," Gloria said. "I suppose you'll have to tell the elders."

"No, not yet. I need to speak to Sam first. I'll do that tomorrow," Ruby said, then paused a moment before saying, "Boy, when it rains, it pours. I suppose Sam told you about the bats."

"What bats?" Gloria asked.

Ruby sighed. "There's a nesting colony of Indiana bats in the meetinghouse attic. It's the mating season, so they can't be removed. The Department of Natural Resources has put a stop to our building project and prohibited us from entering the meetinghouse for three, maybe four, months. Didn't Sam tell you?"

"He didn't say the first thing about it."

"Well, I did ask him to keep it under his hat until we'd lined up another place to worship," Ruby said. "But I just assumed he'd tell you, since you're his parents."

"Apparently, he's kept quite a few things from us," Gloria Gardner said, her voice catching.

"What a day," Ruby said.

"I woke up this morning and everything was wonderful," Gloria said. "Then I got hit by a car, my bike is ruined, my son is a lush, and we can't have church just when I need it the most. I wish I'd never woken up this morning."

"You got hit by a car?" Ruby asked. "How dreadful."

"Hit by a bimbo who was texting and ran a stop sign."

"Oh, Gloria, I'm so sorry. Are you all right?"

"Just sore is all. Nothing broken, thank God. The doctor gave me some pain medicine. I think I'll take one before I go to bed."

"Yes, soak in a nice, warm bath, take a pill, and go to bed," Ruby advised.

Which Gloria did. And she did feel better. She took two pills instead of one, thinking if one pill was good, two would be better. She lay in bed, positively glowing, warmth washing over her body. Except for her knees, where she still felt a residue of pain. She hoped she wouldn't need a knee transplant or replacement, whatever it was they did with knees. She'd like to get her hands on the girl who hit her. Just one minute, just long enough to shake her and smash her phone. She decided to take two more pills, to be on the safe side, so she wouldn't wake up in the morning unable to move her knees.

Falling asleep, she felt at peace. Talking with Ruby must have helped, she thought. She liked Ruby. Ruby always knew what to do. She reminded Gloria of her mother, a wise, kind-hearted Quaker woman. She thought maybe she'd call Ruby in the morning and invite her out to lunch. That was the last thought she had before falling to sleep. Lunch with Ruby and maybe her mother and the girl who hit her. Just the four of them.

27

Herb arrived at the hospital a few minutes after Stacey. He gathered up the twins and hurried inside, where he was met by a young lady in a lab coat who asked if he was Dr. Maxwell.

"Yes, I am," he said, handing her a twin, then reaching into his pocket and retrieving the sandwich bag with the bat inside. "I need you to have this bat tested for rabies. I'd like the results as soon as possible, please."

"Do you want me to take your babies to the nursery, so you can be with your wife?"

"Yes, thank you, I'd appreciate that."

She summoned an aide to help carry the bat and babies. He handed off Ezra and Emma, slung the diaper bag over the young lady's shoulder, kissed each baby good-bye, then hustled through the emergency room doors to be with his wife.

Hospitals would never admit it, but the family members of medical workers went to the front of the line. Stacey was already headed to an operating room, a doctor trailing behind her gurney, talking on his cell phone, assembling a surgery team.

Herb caught up to him as he was finishing his call. "I've got the state's best hand surgeon on her way over," he told Herb. "And a plastic surgeon is coming over to tidy things up. Her hand is pretty mangled. It's amazing the damage a dog bite can inflict. What kind of dog was it?"

"A poodle named Precious. It belonged to her aunt and we inherited it when she died," Herb explained.

"Precious. Wouldn't you know it. Poodles can be vicious little monsters."

"It was eating a dead bat," Herb said. "I brought it with me. The lab is testing it for rabies."

"Now wouldn't that be a nice complication."

"Can I gown up, and watch the operation?" Herb asked.

"Probably not a good idea. Why don't you go back to the waiting room and I'll keep you updated."

Herb returned to the waiting room, sorted through the magazines until he'd found a year-old *Field & Stream*, and began to read about fly-tying and Lyme disease. After reading the article, he was pretty confident he had Lyme disease. He had a tendency toward hypochondria, worrying he had every illness he read about—smallpox, anthrax, ovarian cysts; though he knew the latter was impossible, he occasionally felt painful twinges about where his ovaries would be if he had a pair.

An hour passed. A nurse came out to tell him everything was going well, that the hand surgeon had just arrived and was preparing for surgery. He went to the nursery to check on the twins, who were sound asleep. He spent a half hour there, rocking babies, hoping to ease his mind, then went back down to the emergency waiting room. An hour passed, a nurse emerged to tell him the surgery had begun, that the doctors were hopeful Stacey would regain full use of her hand, but it was too early to tell. There had been extensive damage to the muscles and some smaller bones, and they were worried about fine motor control.

"About another hour, and she'll be out of surgery and in the recovery room. You can see her then," the nurse promised Herb.

Herb had never cared for Precious, even though he was a dog person. But there was something about that dog he'd never quite trusted. He certainly didn't want it around his children any longer. He closed his eyes in thought, wondering who he might give it to, an enemy perhaps, someone evil, with whom Precious could feel a kinship.

28

Sam and Barbara's telephone rang as they were crawling into bed. It had been a long day and they were exhausted.

"Let the answering machine get it. It's probably the Finks," Sam said.

"No, you better get it. It might be one of the boys."

Sam picked up the phone and said hello.

"Get over here quick, something's wrong with your mother," his father said.

"What do you mean something's wrong? What's she doing?"

"Nothing. That's the problem. I can't wake her up."

"We'll be right there," Sam said, then remembered his mother's accident from earlier in the day, though it seemed like a month ago. "When I hang up, call an ambulance."

Charles Gardner felt about medical personnel the same way he felt about hiring someone to work on your house. Why waste your money? Instead, he got a cup, filled it with water from the bathroom tap, and poured it on Gloria's face.

"Can you hear me?" he yelled.

She could indeed hear him, but her answer was garbled and incoherent because there was water in her nose and she was choking and sneezing. When she tried to form words, they wouldn't come, and then she began to panic. She'd watched an *Oprah* show on near-death experiences and suspected she was having one. She felt outside herself, as if there were two of her, one living and one observing the living.

Then she heard Sam and Barbara. What were they doing here? She felt herself lifted from the bed and carried outside to a car. It was dark, the streetlights were smears of little suns in the dark, one after another, and then she heard voices and felt strong, strange hands lift her from the car and put her in a chair. And there were more suns, now constant, and she felt peace cover her like a blanket, just like the people on *Oprah* had talked about.

29

hy's she wet?" Sam asked his father.
"I poured a glass of water on her."
"Why in the world did you do that?"

"It was cheaper than an ambulance. You know what they charge for an ambulance? Eight hundred dollars! Now you tell me why I have to pay eight hundred dollars for an ambulance and an EMT I've already paid for with my taxes. Anyway, she's here, so what difference does it make?"

Sam, Barbara, and Charles Gardner were seated in the hospital emergency room, bickering. First, about the ambulance, then about the DNR shutting down the church.

"I tell you one thing, I wouldn't have stood for it. I'd have climbed up in that attic and killed those bats and not given it a second thought," Charles Gardner said.

The waiting room was full of people trying not to stare at them. There were all kinds of people in an emergency room at eleven o'clock—mothers with sick kids, drunks, druggies, seemingly normal families squabbling about the most curious matters.

It was the squabbling that caught Herb Maxwell's attention. It was coming from behind him. He wanted to turn and stare, but didn't want to be obvious. He rose to his feet, faked a stretch and a yawn, then turned to survey the room as if bored, and saw Sam and Barbara, who also saw him.

They jumped to their feet and hurried over to Herb. "What in the world are you doing here?" Sam asked.

Herb was leery of Sam. Who wouldn't be? No normal man killed a bagful of bats for no good reason.

"Stacey got bit by our dog," he said, leaving out the bat part.

"Where are Emma and Ezra?" Barbara asked.

"They're in the hospital nursery."

"You should have called us," Sam said. "We'd have been happy to watch them."

Fat chance of that, Herb thought.

"Is she going to be all right?" Barbara asked, concerned.

It was hard to believe a woman as kind and thoughtful as Barbara Gardner was involved in the ritual slaying of animals. Herb didn't want to believe it, but he'd seen the bats. Then again, maybe it was all Sam's doing. Maybe Barbara didn't know the first thing about it. Maybe Sam was like those dirty old men who kept girlie magazines hidden in their workbench, their wives never suspecting a thing, until one day they went looking for a pair of needle-nose pliers and found Miss March instead, posed on the hood of a '57 Chevy. Yes, Herb was starting to think Barbara didn't know the first thing about Sam's sordid appetites.

Then again, Herb couldn't be sure. Sure, she was an elementary school librarian, but wouldn't that be the perfect job for a Satan worshipper? Who would ever suspect her?

He wondered if she had a pentagram tattooed on her rump, where no one could see it. He'd read about a family, he couldn't remember where they were from, maybe Wisconsin, who'd been devil worshippers and no one had a clue. The father was a Rotarian, the mother taught Sunday school, the son played Little League, and the daughter was a Girl Scout, but at night they sat in a circle and lit candles to Lucifer. The neighbors hadn't suspected a thing, until one evening the lady across the street knocked on the door to borrow an egg and their secret was out. Yes, now that he thought about it, Barbara was probably right in the thick of it with Sam. In fact, the more Herb thought about it, the more he suspected Barbara had been the one to lure Sam into it. That's the way it usually worked, the crafty woman enticing the not-too-bright, naïve man.

"Is she going to be all right?" Barbara asked a second time.

"Oh, sure, yeah. They're operating on her now. Repairing some tendon damage."

"That must have been some dog bite," Sam said. "What kind of dog was it?"

Why the sudden interest in dogs? Herb wondered. Weren't bats enough? Was he escalating? First, small mammals, but after a while, that not being enough, he'd graduate to larger creatures, gradually, inexorably, working his way up to humans.

"I've got to go now," Herb said, then turned and walked away.

"Poor guy," Sam said as he watched Herb leave. "You can tell he's really worried about Stacey."

"Did he seem a little odd to you?" Barbara asked Sam. "A little distant?"

"Well, of course he did. His wife is being operated on. Did you think he'd be cracking jokes?"

"I suppose you're right."

They returned to sit with Sam's father, who was talking to a young man seated next to him about the Colts. If he were concerned about Gloria, he was doing a wonderful job of hiding it. "Peyton Manning, Peyton Manning, that's all you ever hear. But you watch and see, this Andrew Luck kid will be the best quarterback the Colts ever had. Better than Unitas, better than Manning. Mark my words."

He pointed in the general direction of the retreating Herb Maxwell. "You see that guy there. He's the Colts' doc, and he says Luck is better than any of them. For crying out loud, he's still a kid. He's got ten, maybe fifteen, years ahead of him, and gettin' better every season."

A nurse emerged from the emergency room and called out their name. Sam had to drag his father away from his conversation. The nurse escorted them to a small room, pointed at a couch, and told them the doctor would be right in. A few minutes passed, then the door pushed open and the doctor entered, taking a seat across from the Gardners.

"How's my mother?" Sam asked.

"She's going to be all right, but we need to discuss some kind of treatment program." The doctor paused. "We're starting to see more of this kind of thing among the elderly. It's becoming a real problem."

"What's becoming a problem?" Sam asked. "What's wrong with her?"

"I'm afraid your mother might have a drug abuse problem. She was high on OxyContin. We had to pump out her stomach."

"Oh, Lord, I knew it would come to this," Charles Gardner said. "We'd move to the city and she'd fall in with the wrong crowd and start doing drugs."

"Oh, my, and they gave her OxyContin this morning," Sam said. "A whole bottle full. She was riding her bicycle and got clipped by a car. They gave her OxyContin for the pain. We had no idea she had a problem. How many did she take?"

"Enough to knock her out. It's a good thing your father had the presence of mind to throw water on her."

"Oh, sure, I thought about calling an ambulance, but I knew I had to act quickly," Charles Gardner said.

"Well, I'm glad you got her here as soon as you did. But you take that OxyContin back to the drugstore and have them dispose of it for you. How long has she been abusing prescription medicine?"

"We have no idea," Sam said. "This comes as a shock to all of us."

They waited another hour, then were permitted to see Gloria.

Sam was the first to speak. "Mom, I don't pretend to understand what drove you to this, but I want you to know I love you and am here to help you, not only as your son, but also as your pastor."

"Yes, me, too," Barbara said.

"What were you thinking, taking all those pills?" Charles Gardner said. "That was really stupid."

"How long have you been addicted?" Sam asked.

"I'm not addicted to anything," his mother said.

Denial was often the first sign of addiction.

Sam reached down to hug her. "It's all right, Mom. We're not judging you. We just want to help you."

His voice cracked. It had been a rough day for the Gardner family. First, there were the bats, then his mother's accident, then his brief flirtation with drunkenness, and now the revelation of his mother's addiction to prescription medications. Not to mention Stacey Maxwell getting mauled by her dog.

At least, Sam thought, it can't get any worse.

30

～

The lady from the Department of Natural Resources headed to the meetinghouse early the next morning to check on the bats. She was stuck behind a trash truck, which was working its way down the street, one man driving, another man tossing trash bags into the truck. They reached the meetinghouse lane, the truck stopped, and the man on the back hopped down, then stooped to study one of the bags further. He yelled for the driver to come look. They bent closer to the bag, nudged it open with their feet, then recoiled in disgust, the tosser man finally bending down to pick up what appeared at first glance to be a dead bird. He spread the wings apart and studied it closely, then reached down to pick up the trash bag and pitch it on the truck, and would have if the lady in the DNR truck hadn't yelled at him to stop.

"Hold up there, buster," she called out, approaching the trash truck. "What you got in that bag?"

The tosser man stepped back. "I don't have anything in the bag. It's not my bag. It belongs to them," he said, pointing down the lane at the meetinghouse.

She pulled open the bag, peered inside, then dumped the contents on the ground.

"My gosh, would you look at that?" she said.

The driver was nonplussed. "That's nothing, lady. You ought to see the stuff people throw away. Just yesterday someone threw out a perfectly good TV. I took it home. I got fifteen TVs out in my garage, and all of 'em work just fine. Wouldn't want to buy one, would you?"

She didn't answer, just started sorting through the bats, counting each one. One hundred and seven Indiana bats. All of them dead, smashed to smithereens. She reached for her cell phone and called her boss.

"We've got a crime scene here. A whole colony of bats killed." She paused. "Nope, not dead. Killed. Someone murdered them. I need some help down here."

She began sorting the bats into piles—adult males, adult females, juvenile males, juvenile females—her anger building. Someone would pay for this. She didn't know who, but she was determined to find out.

"Can we go, lady?" the driver asked.

"Just as soon as I get your names, addresses, and telephone numbers. You might be called as witnesses. Let's see some ID, guys."

They showed her their driver's licenses, gave her the information she needed, then went on their way.

A half hour later, the bat specialist with the hairy, scrunched face arrived. He stared at the bats, studying each one.

"Have you talked to anyone?" he asked.

"No, I wanted to wait until you got here."

"Let's start with the pastor."

They pulled their trucks into the meetinghouse parking

lot, walked over to the parsonage, and knocked on the door.

Barbara had already left for work, but Sam was home, freshly showered and sitting down to a bowl of oatmeal. When they knocked, Sam groaned. A visitor was the last thing he wanted. They'd talk his arm off and by the time they left, his oatmeal would be cold and congealed into a hard lump. There was nothing worse than oatmeal gone bad. He thought about not answering the door. It was probably the Finks, wanting to borrow cleaning supplies. Then he'd have to tell them about the bats and the meetinghouse being closed, and they'd whine and moan and rail against big government and how Christians were being discriminated against and how if it were a mosque it wouldn't be closed down. Sam was in no mood to hear it. He sat quietly, not moving, scarcely breathing, trying not to give off any vibes that he was home.

The knocking continued for another minute, then stopped. A moment later he heard voices at his back door, and there was the hairy, scrunched-face bat man, peering through the back door at him.

"Mr. Gardner, we need to talk," he called out.

And with that, Sam's hopes for hot oatmeal were dashed.

31

Sam opened the door and welcomed them into the kitchen.

"I was just sitting down for breakfast. Would you like some oatmeal?"

"No, thank you," said the bat man. "We have a few questions."

"Is it okay if I eat my oatmeal while it's still warm?" Sam asked.

This guy's a monster, the DNR lady thought. *He kills over a hundred bats and all he's thinking about is eating his oatmeal. No sense of shame or guilt. He must be a sociopath. When we start digging, we'll discover he has a long history of animal abuse. Probably killed kittens as a kid.*

"We're here about the bats," the bat man said.

"Yeah, I suspected you were," Sam said between bites. He was growing inordinately fond of oatmeal and made a mental note to thank Mary Ann Drooger the next time he was at the grocery store. If it weren't for her, he'd still be hooked on Cocoa Krispies.

"We need to see inside the meetinghouse," the bat man said.

"Help yourself," Sam said. "If the bats don't mind, I guess I don't, either." He reached in his pocket and gave them a key. "We don't ordinarily keep the place locked, but I figured with the bats needing some peace and quiet, it'd be a good idea to lock it up."

It was all the DNR lady could do not to reach across the table and slap him silly.

"We'll have to ask you not to leave, until we've inspected the meetinghouse," the bat man said.

"Well, I was going to visit my mom, but I suppose it can wait a few more minutes. Shouldn't take you too long to look things over. Right?"

Was it her imagination, or was he toying with them? the DNR lady wondered.

"Don't leave this house," she commanded. "No matter if we're gone five minutes or all day. Stay put. Or we'll slap the cuffs on you and haul you downtown. You're on thin ice, buster."

In her long years of service, she'd learned to deal firmly with sociopathic personalities.

Sam was so shocked he didn't say anything, though after they left, he phoned Barbara and left a message on her voice mail to tell her if he disappeared, she should look for him downtown, in the bowels of the jail. He was beginning to wonder if maybe the Finks were right about big government.

The bat man retrieved a ladder from his DNR truck and carried it into the meetinghouse, propping it against the wall next to the attic access, then eased his way up, quietly lifting the door just enough to peer inside the attic and shine his flashlight into the rafters. His worst fears were realized. Instead of the cluster of bats he'd seen just yesterday, the rafters were bare. He opened the door farther and lifted himself into the attic, then lowered a hand to help the DNR lady in.

"Maybe they moved to another section of the attic," he said quietly. "You start at that end and I'll start over here. Cover every square inch."

They spent a half hour looking for any sign of bats, but even the guano was gone.

"It's like they were never here," the bat man said. "I've never seen anything like it."

"Look at this," the DNR lady said, picking up a two-by-four leaning against a rafter. "This must be what he used. There's blood on it."

"Don't touch it," the bat man said. "It's evidence."

They poked around further. "Look here," the bat man said, shining his light into the rafters. "He caulked the openings shut where the bats got in. What kind of monster would do this?" the bat man said.

"The kind of monster who could invite us into his house and eat oatmeal like he didn't have a care in the world," the DNR lady said. "Let's arrest him."

"Hold on. All we know is that a crime has been committed. We don't have any proof he did it. Not yet anyway. Let's call it in, then go talk to him."

While they waited for their colleagues to arrive, they went back to the parsonage, where they found Sam still seated at the kitchen table, anxious.

"Let's read him his rights," the DNR lady said. "We don't want him whining later that he didn't know his rights."

It surprised most people to learn that DNR officers had arrest powers, just like police officers, and suspects often blurted out their guilt thinking no harm could come of it.

"What do you mean, read me my rights?" Sam screeched. "I haven't done anything."

He wondered if maybe they knew about him getting drunk at Bruno's and were arresting him for public drunkenness, which would pretty well ruin his career as a pastor.

"We just have a few questions to ask you," the bat man said. "Shouldn't take too long at all. You can call your lawyer, if you want, but really you shouldn't need one."

"Call my lawyer? I don't have a lawyer. Owen Stout did our wills, but that was ten years ago and he's back in Harmony. I don't think he'd come all the way up here. I'm not even sure he's still my lawyer. And it's not like I drove or anything. I just had a little too much wine and I'm not used to it. I'm as much against public intoxication as the next man, but I didn't make a scene or attack anyone. At least that I can remember."

"So you're telling me you got drunk, killed a hundred and seven Indiana bats, and don't remember a bit of it," said the DNR lady.

"If I did, I don't remember it," said Sam, wishing he'd never taken that first drink.

32

The DNR rolled in at full force, crawling over the meeting-house and grounds, scouring the trees in search of bats, every now and then casting disgusted looks in the direction of where Sam was seated in a lawn chair under a tree, a burly man beside him, just waiting for an excuse to beat Sam to a bloody pulp. They found a dozen bats, slumbering under the bark in two dead trees next to the meetinghouse, looking shell-shocked.

They allowed Sam one call, which he used to phone Ruby Hopper, who called Barbara, who in turn phoned Owen Stout, who didn't practice criminal law, though he knew someone who did and would phone on Sam's behalf.

They'd showed Sam the bludgeoned bats and he was in shock. One hundred and seven little bat corpses stretched out in rows on a clean white sheet.

"Honest, I didn't do it," he said to the DNR lady.

"The jails are full of people saying the same thing," she snarled. "Put a lid on it, buster."

Barbara and Ruby Hopper arrived within moments of one another. Barbara insisted on Sam's innocence.

"There's no way he could have done it. He was with me the whole day."

They didn't believe her for a minute.

"It could just as easily have been me," Ruby Hopper said. "I knew about the bats. I don't even have an alibi. I spent the whole day at home and didn't see a soul."

"Was it you?" asked the bat man.

"Of course not. I wouldn't do that. I'm just saying I knew about the bats, too, so you can't assume it was Sam."

"Who all knew about the bats?" the bat man asked.

"Hank Withers knew about the bats being in the trees and the building project being postponed," Ruby said. "He called and told me about them. But he didn't know about the bats being in the meetinghouse attic. You didn't find those until the next day."

"I knew," Sam said, "and I called Ruby and told her and she told me not to tell anyone, but I went ahead and told my wife. I tell her everything." Not exactly everything. He'd never told her about having a crush on Gretchen Weber and her French braid. "And I told Bruno, because he told us we could maybe meet at the Catholic church. Let me see, my wife, Ruby, and Bruno. that's it. One of them must have done it."

"I didn't do it," Barbara said.

"Neither did I," added Ruby. And I mentioned it to your mom, but she couldn't have done it. She was in no kind of shape to do anything like that."

"Then it was Bruno," Sam concluded. "You know how those Italians are. He probably thought he was doing us a favor. Sent over someone to take care of things. The guy shows up, whack, whack, whack, problem solved."

"You told your dad," Barbara said to Sam. "Remember, at

the hospital. He said he'd have climbed up in the attic and killed the bats." Her voice trailed off.

Sam was poised to object, then it occurred to him it was exactly something his father would have done. He'd once seen his father kill a whole nest of snakes. Chopped them up with a shovel, quick as you please. And bats weren't much different than snakes on the icky scale. But when had he done it? He hadn't found out until late in the evening, at the hospital, when Sam told him. Had he slipped over during the night? *Men loveth the dark more than the light, because their deeds are evil.* It said that in the Bible, Sam was reasonably sure.

"Could your father have done this?" the DNR lady asked.

"I'm not saying another word," Sam said. "Not one more word."

33

Cleaning the meetinghouse for a hundred dollars a week was the easiest money the Finks had ever made. Sweep the kitchen floor, hit the bathrooms, pick up a stray bulletin or two, wash the windows once or twice a year, kill the occasional colony of bats, and call it a day. But what they loved most was snooping through Sam's office. They'd found a key their first week of cleaning, hidden in the broom closet, hanging on a hook over the door, tried it on the front door, didn't work, then tried it on the office lock, and bingo, they were in. They read his files first, which he hadn't bothered to secure since he locked his office door.

He didn't have many counseling notes on the people at Hope, hadn't been there long enough to learn any good dirt. But there were reams of notes from his counseling sessions at Harmony Friends Meeting, and even though Leonard and Wanda didn't know the people involved, it still made for interesting reading—divorces, addictions of every type, marital spats, love affairs, embezzlement, spiritual struggles. The people at Harmony Friends Meeting had been hard at work.

There were no names, just first initials. Sam had written his insights, his suggested course of action for the counselees, his follow-up, possible outcomes, and months, sometimes years, later, the resolution of the problem. It would have made a great TV show.

"Would you look at this," Leonard had said to Wanda, "not once has he advised them to read the Bible or pray or anything like that. He sent some folks to a marriage counselor, sent a couple of these people to doctors, lined up a lawyer for this guy, gave a few of them a book to read. Here's a man he drove to a treatment center for alcoholism, but no prayer anywhere, no Scripture." Leonard shook his head, dumbfounded. "What kind of minister is he, anyway?"

"I don't trust him," Wanda had said.

Despite their occasional foray into Sam's files, they were finally making some headway at the meetinghouse. The place hadn't had a good going-over in some time. They were working their way through the meetinghouse, room by room. They hadn't counted on the bats. That had set them back a day. Today, they would work on the nursery, now that there were children in the meeting. Though they didn't approve of Herb and Stacey, especially since Hank Withers had told him Herb gave physicals to cheerleaders and probably even saw them naked.

"You watch, one day we'll see counseling notes on them," Wanda had predicted.

They drove to the meetinghouse, turned down the lane, and saw cars and trucks everywhere, all manner of activity.

"There's a meeting and they didn't tell us," Leonard said. "I've just about had it with these people. They leave us out of everything."

"I bet they're holding a meeting about the new building and didn't tell us because they know we're against it," Wanda said. "They're just ramming it through with no regard for our feelings."

There were strangers there, probably county officials, they surmised, studying the site to issue permits.

Sam, Barbara, and Ruby Hopper were standing off to one side, talking to a man and woman.

"What's going on here?" Leonard yelled, waving his arms, walking toward Sam. "This wasn't approved by the church. We gave Hank permission to talk to builders, but that's all."

"What's your name, buster?" the DNR lady asked Leonard.

"What's my name? What do you mean, what's my name? What's your name? And what are you doing here? We didn't agree to build yet. You just pack up and get out of here."

Leonard Fink had been a somewhat passive, henpecked man when Sam had first met him, but in the past year he'd come out of his shell and was well on his way toward becoming a jerk.

"We're here because someone went up in the church attic and massacred a hundred and seven Indiana bats, which are a protected species," the DNR lady fired back. "And when we find out who did it, we're going to hang him high."

Leonard Fink had been clueless most of his life, so feigning it was easy.

"Bats?" he said. "What bats?"

"There were bats in the meetinghouse attic," Sam explained, "and someone killed them."

"Maybe they just left," Leonard said.

"And cleaned up all their poop, then sealed the cracks with caulk on their way out, I suppose," the bat man said.

"Well, don't look at me. I'm just the janitor. We came to clean the nursery today."

"Not today," the DNR lady said. "The meetinghouse is off-limits."

"I'm not meaning to be argumentative," Ruby Hopper said, "but if the bats are dead, and that is most unfortunate, but if they're no longer in the meetinghouse, why can't we use it?"

There was no reason, except that the bat man and the DNR lady were furious and not about ready to let Hope Friends have their meetinghouse back.

"Not until we've finished this investigation," said the bat man. "Right now it's the scene of a crime and off-limits to everyone except DNR personnel."

The DNR lady turned to Sam. "How can we get in touch with your father? As of now, he's our number one suspect."

"He lives right down the street," Leonard said, pointing south. "A green house with cream trim. Two story, with a big front porch. You can't miss it."

34

The DNR people eventually departed, Barbara returned to work, and the Finks slunk away, which left Sam and Ruby by themselves.

"Sam, do you have a moment?" Ruby asked.

Sam glanced at his watch as if there were pressing matters at hand. With the office closed, Sam had nowhere to go and nothing to do, though he certainly didn't want to give that impression to Ruby, lest she think pastors were unnecessary.

"Maybe we can sit on your porch," Ruby said, leading the way across the meetinghouse lawn to Sam's house.

They sat side by side on the porch swing.

"How have you been doing lately, Sam? I know you're under a great deal of stress, having to help your parents as they age. I know you worry about money with Levi in college, and I can't imagine what it would be like to have a child in the army in these dangerous times. You're probably worried sick about him. So how are you doing?"

"I'm holding up," Sam said, even though Ruby's summary of his life had left him feeling a bit anxious.

"Not to mention having to pastor a meeting that is contemplating a building project. Why, I read just the other day that ninety percent of the pastors whose churches build are fired or leave within two years after the project is completed. I can't image the stress you must feel."

"I try to exercise and eat right," Sam said. "I've switched to oatmeal. That's helped a lot."

"Proper diet and exercise are very important," Ruby agreed. "What we take into our bodies has a profound effect on our well-being."

"Amen to that."

"In fact, that's what I wanted to talk about with you. I know when people become anxious and stressed out, it isn't uncommon for them to self-medicate. Some do that with drugs."

Sam thought of his mother, and sadly nodded his head.

"Others turn to alcohol," Ruby continued. "It isn't uncommon and it's nothing to be ashamed of, nevertheless it isn't healthy and only creates more stress and problems in the long run."

"I've seen it happen more times than I can count," Sam said.

"That's why I want to urge you to get help now," Ruby said. "Your mother told me about your, uh, situation yesterday."

"What exactly did she tell you?"

"She told me about your struggle with alcohol," Ruby said. "Of course, we in the meeting had no idea, or we would have approached you before now. Don't get me wrong, your job is not in jeopardy. We, and now I'm speaking on behalf of the meeting—though I haven't shared your condition with anyone—but I'm sure I speak for the meeting when I tell you that we want to help any way we can."

"I don't know where Mom got the idea that I have a drinking problem," Sam said. "Barbara and I had lunch at Bruno's and I had a little too much wine. It was the first time I drank that much, and it will be the last time."

"I'm sorry if I've overstepped the boundaries," Ruby said. "I just wanted to make sure you're okay."

"I appreciate your concern, Ruby. And I'm okay. Honestly, it's Mom I'm worried about. We took her to the hospital yesterday with a drug overdose. The doctor thinks she might have an addiction to prescription drugs."

"Oh, my. Your mother? I never would have guessed it."

"All of us are surprised," Sam said. "Quite frankly, we never saw it coming."

"What are you doing about it?"

"Unfortunately, there isn't much we can do. She refuses to admit she has a problem. Dad's going to make sure all the medicines are locked up, but addicts have a way of getting the drugs they crave."

"I have to say, and I don't mean to be cruel, but I have some misgivings about your mother serving on the building committee knowing she's suffering from an addiction. I want her to focus on getting better. Everything else should be secondary."

"I agree," Sam said. "I think it would be wise to give someone else that responsibility. Perhaps Libby Woodrum could serve."

"I'll approach her about that," Ruby said. "But I'll speak to your mother beforehand. I don't want her to learn this from someone else. Perhaps it will be just the jolt she needs to get help."

Sam nodded in agreement. It was funny how these kinds

of things worked out. As difficult as it had been to tell Ruby about his mother's problem, it was out in the open now. No more hiding it, no more pretending the problem didn't exist. These problems needed to be faced head-on. He felt a flood of warmth toward Ruby Hopper, and reached across and squeezed her hand in gratitude.

"We're so fortunate to have you in the meeting," he told her. "You can't imagine how deeply you are loved by all of us."

35

⌒

Y ou're nuts," Gloria Gardner told Ruby Hopper. "I don't
have a drug problem. It's Sam who has the problem."
She began to weep. "We've discovered our son is an alcoholic."

"Gloria, you've mentioned that before, and I've spoken
with him. I'm almost certain Sam doesn't have a drinking
problem. He explained what happened and I believe him."

"You don't think he's a drunk?"

"No, I don't. I honestly don't," Ruby said. "Now let's talk
about what happened with you. You mustn't abuse your prescription medications. They're very powerful and can be very
dangerous if taken incorrectly. Do you have someone who can
oversee your medications?"

"I'm not a half-wit. I only took four of those pills because
my knees hurt and I thought they were like aspirin. I know better now. I don't even have them anymore. Charles took them
back to the drugstore."

"That's good. Sam and I were very concerned about you."
Ruby began to chuckle. "In fact, we were so worried, we were
going to replace you on the building committee."

"Oh, no," Gloria said. "I want a woman on that committee. I don't want a bunch of men designing the new meetinghouse kitchen. Can you see Wayne Newby planning out a kitchen?"

"Hadn't thought of that," Ruby said. "We don't want that, do we? Well, I guess it's a moot point, since you're not an addict. We'll just keep you on the committee. But please be careful with your medicine in the future."

Ruby hesitated.

"What else is it?" Gloria asked, sensing Ruby's unease.

"It's about the bats in the meetinghouse attic. You remember my telling you about them?"

"Yes, I remember."

"Someone killed them," Ruby said. "One hundred and seven of them. Whoever did it cleaned up all the guano and caulked the cracks so they couldn't get back in. The DNR is investigating. They're treating the meetinghouse as a crime scene and we can't go in. Someone is going to be in real trouble."

"Oh, that's dreadful," Gloria Gardner said. "Who would do such a thing?"

"That's just it. Only a few people knew about the bats. Me, you, Sam, Barbara; and Sam and Barbara told Charles, who unfortunately said that if it were up to him, he'd kill the bats. The DNR knows he said that, and they might want to talk with him. Do you think he might have done such a thing?"

She was going to say of course not, then remembered the time he'd found a nest of mice in their basement and he'd taken off his boot and smashed them flat. Then there were those snakes.

"I don't think he would," she said, but there was a hint of doubt in her voice.

Ruby sighed. "Well, I hope he has a good alibi."

The thought of such carnage left them discouraged, so Ruby suggested they spend some time designing the new meeting-house kitchen. They phoned Hank Withers to ask how big the kitchen was going to be, in the event Hank was able to design a new addition that didn't require the removal of trees and the meeting approved the building project.

"Fourteen feet wide and twenty-three feet long," he said. "I want it to follow the golden ratio."

"I have no idea what the golden ratio is, but I'll take your word that it's important," Ruby said.

Hank proceeded to launch into a lecture on the ancient principles of architecture, which Ruby cut off by thanking Hank for the information and hanging up the phone.

It was a beautiful day, so they went outside to the driveway, measured off an area fourteen by twenty-three, and imagined where everything might go—doors, windows, sinks, cabinets, refrigerators, stoves, and freezers. It was like being a child again and playing with a dollhouse.

The DNR lady arrived just as they finished, parking her DNR truck on top of their kitchen plans.

"Is this the home of Charles Gardner?" she asked.

"My husband didn't kill those bats, so you just get right back in your little green truck and scoot on out of here," Gloria said.

"I will talk to your husband if I want to." It might have been the worst possible thing the DNR lady could have said.

"Not without an attorney present you won't," said Gloria, who had watched thousands of hours of television shows about lawyers and judges and police officers and had such matters down pat.

"I'll be back. And your husband better be here when I return."

Gloria Gardner had not been the president of the Friendly Women's Circle for fourteen years without learning how to deal with headstrong women. She wasn't one to cave in at the first sign of rebellion.

"You are trespassing on our property. You need to leave right now, and don't come back until you have proof my husband did something illegal."

Ruby Hopper watched, enthralled. For the past dozen years, she had been looking for a strong woman to succeed her as the clerk of Hope Friends Meeting, a capable woman who didn't take guff from anyone, who could stand her ground. She had been grooming Norma Withers, who had unfortunately been stricken with Alzheimer's and was out of the running. She had thought Gloria Gardner was too passive, but now had second thoughts.

They watched the DNR lady back out of the driveway.

"I believe you'll do just fine on the building committee," Ruby said to Gloria, slipping her arm around her. "Just fine."

36

Herb and Stacey Maxwell were back home from the hospital, the insurance company having given her the heave-ho a scant three hours after her surgery. Her parents had arrived to watch the twins, and Stacey and Herb were lying in bed, fatigued.

"The more I think about it, the more I don't think Sam could have killed those bats," Stacey said. "He seems too passive."

"That's what they always say about those guys who bury people in their crawlspace," Herb said. "He was real quiet. He kept to himself."

"Are we going back there?"

"I don't know. It's too creepy for me."

"I'm glad the test for rabies came back negative," Stacey said.

"There is that," Herb agreed.

"You know, maybe no one in the meeting had anything to do with it," Stacey said. "Maybe someone dumped the bats there. Besides, we'd agreed to try the meeting for three months, and I think we should stick with that."

"Okay, but if I find out anyone in the meeting had anything to do with it, I'm out of there," Herb said. "I don't think I could go to church with someone who did something like that."

They discussed what to do about Precious, who had been snarling around ever since they had gotten home. While locked in the garage, he had chewed a tire off their lawn mower and peed on Herb's golf clubs.

"I think we need to euthanize that dog," Herb said. "It's a menace."

"So you couldn't attend church with someone who killed bats, but you want to kill our dog? How is that any different?"

"There's a big difference. It's not like I want to beat our dog to death, like someone did those bats. I want to humanely put it to sleep so it can go to heaven and be happy with Jesus."

"I didn't think you believed in heaven," Stacey pointed out.

Herb not believing in heaven had been the source of several vigorous discussions over the years.

"If I say I believe in heaven, can we put Precious to sleep?"

"No, you can't say you believe in something just because it will benefit you," Stacey said.

"Yes, that would be like believing in Jesus so you could go to heaven when you die, wouldn't it?"

Sometimes she thought Herb should have been the lawyer.

Herb not believing in heaven is the other thing that had gotten them in trouble at their previous church. He had let it slip in a Sunday school class, and the teacher ratted him out to the pastor, who phoned Herb to discuss the dangers of free thought, and suggested Herb might be happier elsewhere, especially if he weren't going to tithe.

This all came back to Herb. "You know," he told Stacey,

"now that I think about it, even if Sam did kill those bats, I'd still prefer going to Hope Meeting than to our old church."

"Me, too."

"But we do have to do something about that dog. I know you promised your aunt we'd take it, but it's irresponsible to have a dangerous dog in the same house with children. Maybe your parents will take the dog. It belonged to your mother's sister, after all."

"My mother and her sister never got along very well," Stacey reminded him. "Besides, she hates Precious."

"I hate Precious. Why does my hating Precious not count, but your mother hating Precious does?"

"Stop badgering me. I'm going to sleep."

They fell asleep, listening to her parents watch an infomercial about a ladder that fit inside the trunk of a car, then unfolded to reach the top of the Empire State Building, and that was so light a little old lady could carry it up three flights of stairs. Herb had bought one of the ladders the year before and Precious had peed on that, too.

37

Across town, Leonard and Wanda Fink were seated in their living room watching *Lester Hickam's Revival Hour and Variety Show*. Lester Hickam was on Channel 40, every night at 10 p.m., and was accepting donations at P.O. Box 01777 in Chattanooga, Tennessee.

"It is a mystery to me that a man like Lester Hickam has to struggle to stay on the air, while evildoers have all the money they want," Leonard Fink said. "Fornicators, pornographers, adulterers, Masons, Democrats. They're all walking around in tall cotton, and Brother Hickam has to plead for money. I don't understand it."

Wanda wasn't her usual spouting, hateful self. She was preoccupied, worrying about the bats.

"You don't suppose we'll get in trouble?" she asked Leonard.

"Number one. It's our job to keep the meetinghouse clean. Rats with wings, that's all bats are. If the meetinghouse had been full of rats, wouldn't they expect us to set rat traps? Of course they would. We were just doing our job.

"Number two," Leonard continued. "This is a perfect example of big government nosing in where it doesn't belong. We can either do what they say, or we can resist their unlawful intrusion into our religious freedoms. What we do in our meetinghouse is none of the government's business. Period."

"I guess I didn't look at it that way," Wanda said. "But you're right. They might as well be telling us how to worship."

"That's my point exactly. That's why I didn't tell that DNR lady what I had done. I won't cooperate in any effort to rob me of my freedoms."

Wanda was seeing Leonard in a new light. He had never been this forceful, this dynamic, before. She had been nagging him for years to be the head of their household, but he always held back. Had always been a little too timid. She liked the new Leonard. The Leonard who grabbed a board and smashed bats. The Leonard who stood up to big government. The Leonard who squared off against Hank Withers and didn't let him get his way on everything.

"You need to run for public office," she told him. "This country needs people like you."

"Funny you should mention that. I've been thinking about running for the school board."

They fell silent, contemplating Leonard's future and watching Lester Hickam. He was preaching about the seven-headed beast, moving about the stage from one flannelgraph to another, showing how the end of the world would unfold. Flames here, earthquakes there, plane crashes, car wrecks, folks flying naked through the sky on their way to heaven.

Leonard sighed wistfully. "Won't that be something?"

"There'll be a lot of folks wishing they'd listened to us, starting with Sam Gardner. You know, when I told him about

Lester Hickam and the end days, he just laughed." Wanda shook her head, mystified.

"I do wish I had taken that two-by-four with me, though," Leonard said, as if not hearing her.

"What?"

"The two-by-four I killed those bats with. I left it up in the attic. If the police check it for fingerprints, I suppose they could trace it back to me. Like they do on TV."

Wanda blanched. "You don't think that will happen, do you?"

Leonard thought a bit longer. "No, I don't see how. They don't have my fingerprints. I wasn't in the army or anything like that."

His lack of military service was a great embarrassment to Leonard. He'd registered for the draft but had been rejected because of a bowel condition causing explosive diarrhea. While many of his classmates were in southeast Asia, Leonard was at home in the bathroom. It was something he didn't talk about much.

He and Wanda had met in a country music bar when they were twenty-one. They didn't like thinking about that now. When people asked how they'd met, they said they had been introduced by a mutual friend, but never mentioned it was in a bar and that Leonard, depressed about his bowel condition, was drunker than a monkey. It was the summer of 1970, Conway Twitty's "Hello Darlin'" was playing on the jukebox, and Wanda asked Leonard to dance. Then they went outside for some fresh air and he kissed her and they stumbled back to her apartment and did some other things and three months later they were married. They rented a trailer at the edge of the city and Wanda got a job at Kmart and Leonard's dad got him a job at General Motors in engine assembly. Wanda was pregnant, but miscarried and there were no more children after that, which made people sad until they got to know Wanda and Leonard; then they realized it was for the best.

They moved to Hope in 1974, Wanda got a job at the hospital, working in the laundry, and on the weekends they hit the bars. In 1982, Lester Hickam came to the city for a revival, and Wanda's sister invited them to attend so Lester Hickam could lay his hands on Wanda's belly and make her conceive, so they went and were saved. Brother Lester encouraged them to find a church home in their town. Somewhere in Hope was a church with no idea what was headed their way. It turned out to be Hope Friends, which they began attending and were soon making a nuisance of themselves. They were the kind of Christians who despised what they had once been and those who still were. Though the other members of Hope Meeting were straitlaced, to Wanda and Leonard they were the worst of sinners, the lukewarm, neither cold nor hot, so God would spew them out of his mouth, but not before warning them, which is why God had sent Wanda and Leonard there, except that no one listened to them.

There were many times Wanda and Leonard had wanted to leave, had wanted to find a church more to their liking, but realized that was Satan talking, realized God wanted them right where they were, lest the people of Hope Meeting backslide entirely. They had been invited to leave several times over the years but had resisted the temptation. God wanted them there, even if it made everyone miserable, which it did.

"Yes," Leonard said, clicking off the television when *Lester Hickam's Revival Hour and Variety Show* came to an end, "I think God is calling me to run for the school board."

38

The DNR didn't arrest Charles Gardner the next day, though the meetinghouse remained closed. Sam phoned the Our Lady of Hope Catholic Church and spoke with the priest, who seemed uncomfortable with the idea of housing a congregation of bat killers.

"We've had our share of bad publicity in recent years," the priest said. "We're trying to avoid any further embarrassment. Word is getting out about what happened at your meetinghouse and, quite frankly, we don't need the negative association. I'm sorry."

Sam hadn't even considered the Catholics would say no. They were two days away from meeting for worship with no place to meet. Now word was getting out about what had happened, and it would kill the modest growth they'd been enjoying. No one wanted to attend church with a bat killer. That was how serial killers got their start.

For the first time, Sam fully realized the mess they were in. Why did things like this always happen in the churches he pastored? Everything would be going along well, then someone would do something stupid. At Harmony Meeting, it was always Dale Hinshaw, who would stand on Christmas or Easter—when they had the most visitors—and rail at people about hell and how from what he could tell, a good number of the people present that morning were going there.

The thought of his church dying depressed Sam, so he decided to eat out and walked the three blocks to Bruno's. It was Spaghetti Day, all the spaghetti you could eat for $5.99, so he had to wait a few minutes for a table. Bruno worked the room, chatting with his customers, calling out greetings to those he knew, and generating goodwill. Sam thought Bruno would have made a good pastor.

"How is Sam today?" Bruno asked, taking a seat across from him. "And why isn't your lovely wife with you?"

"She's working today. And I've been better."

"What's your problem?"

"I spoke with your priest this morning and they're unwilling to let us meet there," Sam said. "I don't know what to do. We only have another day to find a place, because it'll take another day to let everyone know."

"That's a real problem you've got," Bruno said. "Hey, how about holding your church service outside? It's supposed to be a beautiful weekend."

"That might work this Sunday, but we can't count on good weather every weekend. Besides, the DNR doesn't want us around the trees where the bats are living. We're in enough trouble as it is with the DNR. I don't want to make them more angry."

"Why is the DNR angry with you? What did you do to them?"

"I didn't do anything," Sam said. "But someone got up in the meetinghouse attic and killed a hundred and seven bats that were up there. Beat their brains out with a two-by-four. So now we're in real trouble."

"Who would do that?"

"I have no idea."

He didn't tell Bruno that for a while he had suspected him of sending a hit man over to knock off the bats.

"In Malaysia they eat bats," Bruno said. "Maybe someone wanted to eat them. Do you have any Malaysians in your church?"

Sam thought of all their recent attenders.

"No, we haven't had any Malaysians show up."

Sam had been hoping someone from a minority would begin attending Hope Friends—an African American, or a Hispanic, or even a Chinese family—so he could brag to other pastors that he pastored a multiracial church. Alas, everyone was pale as a ghost, just like him.

"Do you have any idiots in your church? 'Cause it would take a real idiot to do something like that."

As soon as Bruno said that, the Finks came to mind, but he dismissed the idea just as quickly. Leonard Fink didn't have it in him. Besides, it wasn't Leonard's style to act on his own. He'd have notified the trustees instead, maybe held a special prayer meeting, perhaps have asked Sam to preach a sermon series on the Bible and mammals. As for Wanda, she was mean enough, but not that industrious. Killing bats and cleaning up their mess would have been too much work. They were looking for someone who was both psychotic and hardworking. She was the former, but clearly not the latter.

"How about you meet with the Methodists?" Bruno suggested. "Maybe combine your churches for three months?"

Sam shook his head no. The Methodist pastor was a real go-getter, probably the best preacher in town. Sam didn't want his congregation listening to her and being tempted toward Methodism.

"You know," Bruno said, looking around the restaurant, "we don't open on Sundays until noon. If you wanted to meet here, you could. Just so long as you didn't mind a little noise back in the kitchen. I know you Quakers like things quiet."

That was an intriguing thought. Holding church in a restaurant. The idea appealed to Sam, in an offbeat sort of way. There were people who went to restaurants who felt intimidated by church buildings. He wondered how the elders would feel about it.

"What would you charge?" Sam asked.

"Charge? I wouldn't charge anything," Bruno said. "I have to turn the lights on anyway. Maybe some of you will stay for Sunday dinner and I'll come out ahead."

"Let me run it by the meeting. But if they agree, could we start this Sunday?"

"It's fine by me. Let me get you a key."

His own key! Sam hadn't been given a key to the meetinghouse in Harmony until his second year there, when Dale Hinshaw had finally consented to having a key made for Sam. Even then, Sam had to sign for it, pledging a solemn oath he would never duplicate it. Then he had to pay the seventy-nine cents Uly Grant charged to copy a key.

They talked a bit longer, working out the details. Sam finished his lunch, Bruno showed him where the light switches and thermostat were, and Sam left, his faith in humanity restored. And to think he hadn't trusted Bruno when they'd first met. Funny how things turned out, he thought, walking home. Why is it, he wondered, that sometimes it was the folks you trusted the least who ended up caring the most?

39

The elders met in an emergency meeting that evening at Ruby Hopper's house. Ruby fed them rhubarb strawberry pie, then shared the sordid details of the week, informing them there was a bat killer loose in the meeting, that the DNR was hot on his trail, and that the meetinghouse would be closed for the next three months, maybe four.

"What makes you so sure it's a he?" Wayne Newby said. "It could have been a she. Granted, most of your bat killers are he's, but it pays to keep an open mind about such things."

"Point well taken," Ruby said. "The three she's who knew were myself, Barbara Gardner, and Gloria Gardner. I know I didn't do it. And Barbara and Gloria said they didn't do it."

"Do you believe them?" Wayne asked, oblivious to Sam's presence.

"Yes, I do," Ruby said.

"Who else knew about the bats?" Wayne persisted.

"Sam, Hank, and Charles Gardner," Ruby answered.

"Sam wouldn't have done it," Wayne said. "He doesn't have the stomach for violence."

"I didn't do it," Hank Withers said. "I didn't even know they were in the attic. I just thought they were in the trees."

"Then that leaves Charles Gardner. It must have been him. Are we turning him in to the police?" Wayne asked.

"He says he didn't do it," Sam said.

"Well, of course that's what he says. You don't think he'd come right out and admit to it, do you?" Wayne said.

"I have to agree with Wayne," Hank said. "I'm betting it was Charles."

Sam would have defended his father, except that he thought it was a remote possibility, given his father's history with various rodents.

"We may never know who did it," Ruby said, deftly changing the subject. "But there are more pressing issues. We have nowhere to meet for worship this Sunday. Sam has a proposal he'd like to make."

"I was eating lunch at Bruno's today," Sam began. "And I—"

"What did you have?" Wilson Roberts interrupted. "I generally get the lasagna."

"Spaghetti," Sam said. "It was Spaghetti Day. So I was there today and—"

"I was stationed in Italy for a year when I was in the army," Hank Withers recalled. "You wouldn't believe the food they had over there. Not that anything is wrong with Bruno's. I think he does a great job."

"—and I was telling Bruno about our situation," Sam continued, speaking quickly so no one could interrupt him, "and he offered to let us meet in his restaurant, so long as we have everything straightened up by eleven thirty."

"Well, that won't work," Wilson Roberts said. "We don't end worship until eleven thirty, then we eat our pie."

"We would have to start worship earlier," Sam said.

"That sounds like a lot of trouble," Wilson said.

"Anything we do is going to present a challenge," Sam pointed out. "We're going to have to be flexible."

"Is Bruno willing to feed us?" Wilson asked. "I think he ought to at least give us something to eat."

"It doesn't work that way," Ruby said. "It's not like we're doing him a favor by meeting there. He's doing us a favor. So no, he won't be feeding us."

"Can we still have our pies?" Wilson asked.

It had become evident to Sam that Wilson stuck with Christianity largely for the desserts. He couldn't wait until some of the newer people became eligible to serve as elders.

"Bruno serves wine. Is that a problem?" Hank asked.

Ruby hesitated, recalling Sam's misadventure earlier in the week. "Well, just because he serves wine doesn't mean we have to drink it during worship."

"What'll we do about music?" Wilson asked. "We have to have a piano."

"Norma bought one of those electronic keyboards a couple years ago," Hank Withers said. "We can use that."

"My niece Gretchen plays the guitar," Ruby Hopper said. "Perhaps she'd be willing to lead our music."

Oh, Lord, not Gretchen Weber, Sam thought. He had enough difficulties without being tempted by Gretchen Weber and her French braid.

"I'm sure we can come up with something," Sam said. "I don't want to press you, but we need to make a decision and start getting word out to folks."

"Well, maybe we can meet there this Sunday and see how it works," Hank said. "If it doesn't work out, we can find somewhere else. But I'd say we don't have much of a choice at this late hour."

"Agreed," said Wilson. "So long as we can bring in our pies."

"Then I suggest we change our meeting for worship to nine thirty," Ruby said. "That'll give us an hour to worship, a half hour for fellowship, and a half hour to get the restaurant ready for business. Sam, can you check with Bruno and see if it's all right if we bring in some pies for our fellowship time?"

"Or perhaps we can ask Bruno if we could purchase some desserts from him," Sam suggested. "Maybe some cannoli or some tiramisu or biscotti?" Eating at Bruno's had broadened Sam's diet.

"Better yet," Ruby said.

"I'd still like a piece of pie," Wilson said.

"Wilson, dear, we all need to sacrifice during this time," Ruby said. "So do Friends approve us gathering at Bruno's for meeting for worship at nine thirty and offering to buy desserts from Bruno?"

"So long as we can change locations if it doesn't work for us," Hank said.

"Of course," Ruby said.

"Approved," the elders rumbled.

"I still wish we could have pie," Wilson said.

Ruby sighed. She couldn't wait until Gloria Gardner took her place.

40

Sam worked the phones all day Saturday, calling people to let them know worship would be held at Bruno's. By then, word had gotten out about the bats, and people had questions and some even voiced their suspicion, most of them centering on Charles Gardner.

He didn't have a phone number for Chris and Kelly, so he phoned Janet Woodrum, the librarian in Harmony, who asked her boyfriend, Pastor Matt of the church where Chris and Kelly used to attend. A few minutes later, Janet called back with a number, which Sam dialed. Chris picked up on the second ring.

Sam told her about the bats and the meetinghouse being closed, then informed her they'd be meeting at Bruno's at nine thirty. "Feel free to invite a friend," Sam added.

"Do you need me to help with the phone calls?" Chris offered.

"I only have a few more to make," Sam said. "But if you want to call Dan and Libby Woodrum, that would be helpful." He gave Chris their phone number.

"We know Dan and Libby from Harmony," Chris said. "They came to our church when they would visit their daughter."

"Wonderful people," said Sam.

"Yes, we've really enjoyed getting to know them."

Sam thanked Chris for her help, then called Wanda and Leonard Fink, albeit reluctantly. What if they moved from place to place each Sunday, never telling the Finks? He smiled thinking about it, then remembered he was their pastor and it was his responsibility to be gracious, so he called them. Wanda answered the phone, Sam explained the situation, and told her they'd be meeting at Bruno's.

"He sells wine, you know," Wanda said. "I'm not sure that's a place Leonard and I would feel comfortable in. We might not be there."

That prospect gladdened Sam's heart as nothing else had in the past week.

"I understand," Sam said. "We'll miss you, but I wouldn't dream of asking you to violate your conscience."

Wanda ranted for a minute or two about wine, then brought up the subject of Chris and Kelly attending the meeting, wanting to know what Sam was going to do about it. "I've already told them how I feel about it. Hate the sin and love the sinner, that's what I told them."

"I bet they felt very loved when you told them that," Sam said.

"Who's that on the phone?" Leonard yelled from the background.

"It's Sam. He's calling to tell us that we're meeting at Bruno's to worship this Sunday."

"Not me," Leonard said. "They serve alcohol there."

"We won't be there," Wanda said.

"Well, okay. We'll let you know if we meet somewhere else," Sam said, trying his best not to sound delighted.

Sam had never been one of those pastors who saw the hand of God in every little thing. Some things, good and bad, just happened. Like bats in the attic. They just happened. A random act of nature. But now that Wanda and Leonard weren't joining them at Bruno's, he began to see the hand of God at work. Maybe those bats were a gift from God, after all.

41

Sam decided that rather than calling Herb and Stacey Maxwell, he would walk over to see them. They were home, it being a Saturday. Stacey met him at the door, her hand wrapped in a bandage as big as a softball. In the chaos of the past few days, Sam had forgotten all about Stacey being bitten by their dog.

"I've come to pay a pastoral visit," Sam said. "I wanted to give you a few days for things to settle down before I dropped in."

She invited him inside. "I'm glad you stopped by," she said. "Hey, Herb, Sam from the church is here."

Herb appeared down the hallway from a bedroom, carrying both babies. "Got them changed," he said, handing one off to Stacey. He turned to Sam and shook his hand. "I think Stacey got bit by the dog to get out of changing diapers."

Sam wondered if Herb had washed his hands after changing the dirty diapers. He hadn't heard the water run. Doctors were notorious for not washing their hands, spreading germs from one patient to another. He made a mental note not to touch his hands to his face until he got home and could wash them.

"Have a seat," Herb said, gesturing toward a rocking chair.

"So tell me all about your dog bite," Sam said, settling in the chair.

"Well, it's quite an interesting story," Stacey said. "That somewhat involves you."

"Oh?" Sam shifted in the chair, uneasy.

"Our dog got out and by the time I found him, he was at the end of the meetinghouse lane, tearing into a trash bag. In the process of pulling him away, he bit my hand."

"I'm sorry," Sam said. "I always put my trash bags in trash cans, but it sounds like one of them got knocked over."

"No, this bag was just sitting on the ground," Stacey said. "There weren't any trash cans there. The bag was full of dead bats."

"Bats?" Sam was starting to hate that word.

"Yes, bunches of bats, all of them dead. Our dog had one in his mouth and when I tried to take it away from him, he bit me."

"Dogs will do that," Sam said, hoping to steer the conversation toward dogs and away from bats. "What kind of dog do you have? You told me once, but I forgot."

"A poodle. We don't have it anymore. We gave it to Stacey's mom and dad."

"I wonder what a bag of bats was doing at the end of the meetinghouse drive," Stacey mused aloud, digging for information.

"They were up in the meetinghouse attic, but someone killed them and left them at the end of the driveway. That's what I've come to tell you. The DNR has closed down our meetinghouse so they can investigate, and until they're done, we'll be meeting at Bruno's."

"Do you have any idea who might have done such a thing?

I mean, that's pretty sick," Stacey said. "Whoever would do that needs therapy."

"No idea," Sam said. "But we have people working on it, and when we find out who it was, they'll be dealt with in an appropriate manner." He was trying to sound professional, as if he himself were heading up a multistate investigation and wouldn't sleep until the perpetrator was deep in the bowels of a prison, undergoing electroshock therapy. Even if it was his dad.

"Here's the deal," said Herb, cutting to the chase. "Seeing those dead bats weirded us out. At first, we thought maybe you or Barbara had something to do with it and we weren't going to attend any longer. But after things settled down, and we thought about it further, we decided it didn't seem like something you'd do—"

"Oh, no, we'd never do something like that," Sam said.

"So we're going to keep coming," Herb continued. "We're making a three-month commitment, then will assess whether or not to make Hope Friends our church home."

"We like that you're not a screamer," Stacey said. "The church we previously attended had a pastor who screamed a lot."

"And we like that you seem open to gays and lesbians," Herb said. "We noticed the two women who seem to be a couple, and people seem to treat them very kindly. That matters a lot to us. We don't want to raise our children in a church that excludes gay people."

"That's Chris and Kelly," Sam said. "I married them, back before it was legal. Got fired for it. That's how I ended up in Hope." He smiled modestly, as if marrying Chris and Kelly had been his idea all along, and not an accident.

Three months. He had three months to rope Herb and Stacey into staying. The bat thing wouldn't help. Who wanted to attend church with a bat-killing psycho? They needed to find out who did it, turn him over to the police, apologize to the DNR, make a donation to the Sierra Club, and move on.

"I'm sorry you were hurt," Sam said. That was a pastor's life, having to apologize for things he hadn't done. "If there's anything we can do to help, please call." He gave them his cell phone number, then fussed over the babies, getting them to smile. He wished his sons would get on the ball, get married, and give him grandchildren to love on.

He was beginning to like Herb and Stacey. He hoped they stayed. The thing was, every other facet of their lives seemed so perfect, so professional. They were accustomed to excellence. Hope Meeting had something to offer, but it wasn't perfection. It wasn't like the churches on TV that had screens that rolled down from the ceiling and cushioned chairs and coffee bars, where the pastor ran things like a CEO and hired people to help him, instead of having to rely on volunteers he couldn't fire when they made mistakes, which they invariably did, because they were human. Somewhere in Herb and Stacey's heads lurked an image of the perfect church, and Sam was afraid Hope Meeting wasn't it.

He thought about it, walking home. It had been like this the entire thirty years he'd been a pastor. You worked hard, did your best to model Jesus, cultivate relationships, did all you could to make the church a warm, hospitable place, and all it took was one nimrod to spoil it for everyone. Why could pastors be fired, but members couldn't? Sam dreamed often of summoning certain members to his office, offering them a chair, folding his hands on the desk, looking across the desk at them and saying, "I'm sorry, but it appears we're not a good fit. We're going to have to let you go." And then they would actually have to go. They couldn't stick around just to spite him. They couldn't whine to the elders and demand he be fired. They couldn't sabotage every new program the church undertook. They just had to get their cushion from the pew, clear out their stuff from their mail slot in the hallway, turn in their name tag, and never come back.

The thought delighted him, and by the time he got home he was positively giddy with joy.

42

B ut why do they think I had anything to do with it?" Charles Gardner griped to his wife. "I didn't touch those bats."

"All I know is that when you and Sam and Barbara were at the hospital and you found out about the bats in the meetinghouse, you said something to the effect that you would have gone up in the attic and killed the bats without a second thought."

"So how did the DNR find out about that?" Charles asked.

"I guess Barbara mentioned it to Sam and a woman from the DNR heard her say it and here we are," Gloria said. "But I'm certain Barbara wasn't trying to get you in trouble. They were just trying to think of everyone who knew anything about the bats. That's all. They just want to eliminate suspects."

"My own daughter-in-law threw me under the bus," Charles grumbled.

"You don't exactly have a good record when it comes to this sort of thing. Remember the snakes you killed, and all those mice that one time?"

"That's different, and you know it."

"Well, did you say you would have killed the bats?" Gloria asked.

"Sure I said it, but I didn't mean it."

"Then you shouldn't have said it," Gloria said. "I've been telling you for years that you don't have to say every thought that pops into your head. And now you're in trouble."

"I oughta be able to tell my own family I'm going to kill something without them telling the police. There's no loyalty these days."

He sat silently, brooding.

"You don't suppose they'll arrest me, do you?" he asked.

"Who knows. We're all the time reading in the paper about these people who get sent to jail for twenty years, then they find out they didn't do it."

Charles groaned. "Twenty years in jail. I'll be nearly a hundred years old."

"On the upside, you'll get free medical care," Gloria pointed out.

"We never should have moved here. This never would've happened if we'd stayed put in Harmony."

"You're the one who wanted to move," Gloria said. "I didn't want to move. I wanted to stay home where our friends were. But no, you had to move. Now here we are, you're headed to jail, and I'll have to take care of this big old heap all by myself."

They spent the rest of the day hissing at one another, before finally deciding it was Sam's fault for not keeping a tighter rein on the members of the meeting.

"He's too easy on them," Charles said. "If he put the fear of God in them now and then, they wouldn't pull stunts like this."

"I've got half a mind not to go there anymore," Gloria said. "Church in a restaurant. You can't have church in a restaurant. What are they thinking?"

"And we're going to go there, and the whole time everyone's

going to be looking at me thinking I'm a bat killer," Charles said. "I'll show them. I just won't go."

With their minds made up, they ate supper, then settled in to see a rerun of *The Lawrence Welk Show* and watched as the six Semonski Sisters—Diane, Donna, Joanne, Valerie, Audrey, and Michelle—sang "Cuanto La Gusta."

"We're old enough to be their parents," Charles said. "Why didn't we have daughters?"

They sat in their recliners, contemplating life as the parents of the famous Semonski Sisters, living in Palm Beach or Rancho del Mirage or wherever it was the parents of famous singers lived.

"Kids like that, I bet they bought their parents a brand-new house," Charles said.

"I wonder what happened to the Semonskis?" Gloria wondered aloud. "You don't hear much about them anymore."

"Yeah, it's funny how you can go from being stars on *The Lawrence Welk Show*, then just fall off the face of the earth."

They pondered the fleeting nature of fame, then watched a rerun of *Gunsmoke*.

"I wonder why Matt and Kitty never got married?" Charles said.

"Maybe he was gay," Gloria mused.

"Don't be silly. People weren't gay back then."

"Sure they were," Gloria said. "They just didn't talk about it."

"Well, Marshal Dillon wasn't one of them," Charles said. "Maybe Doc was, but not Matt."

They squabbled a bit longer, then brushed their teeth and went to bed, setting their alarm clock out of pure habit, so as to wake up in time for church, even though they weren't going.

43

In all his years of pastoring, Sam had never preached in a restaurant, so he and Barbara woke up on Sunday morning earlier than usual, ate breakfast, showered, and were out the door two hours before worship began. Sam hung a sign on the meetinghouse door informing anyone who showed up that they were worshipping at Bruno's.

"You realize, don't you," Barbara pointed out, "that if any visitors show up here, it's because they don't know we've changed locations. And if they don't know we've changed locations, they probably don't know we're starting an hour earlier. So by the time they get here, read the sign, and get over to Bruno's, worship will be over."

"Don't hand me another problem," Sam said. "I have enough on my mind as it is."

They walked to Bruno's, let themselves in the front door, pushed the tables to the side, and arranged the chairs into rows. That didn't look right. Besides, when they ate dessert, they'd need the tables, so they pulled the tables back into place and grouped the chairs around them. There were candles on the tables, which looked too Catholic for Sam's taste, so they gathered them up and sat them on the counter next to the cash register.

Hank and Norma Withers arrived with the keyboard and plugged it in next to the salad bar. Norma sat down and began playing. Since her Alzheimer's, her repertoire had shrunk. She knew "The Old Rugged Cross," "Amazing Grace," and "I've Got You Under My Skin," which she'd heard Frank Sinatra sing in 1974 when she had accompanied Hank to an architects' convention in Chicago. She thought it might make a nice song for the offering.

Bruno arrived a half hour before worship and began clattering the pots and pans in the kitchen. Before long, the smell of food permeated the restaurant. People began rolling in—most of the regulars except for the Finks, plus Herb and Stacey carrying Ezra and Emma, several new attenders, and Chris and Kelly with two of their friends. Sam wondered if their friends were gay. He wished there were a way to tell. Gay people were tricky that way, most of them looked regular, like everyone else. He hugged Chris and Kelly. Barbara had once expressed concerns about his hugging attractive young women, but had told him he could hug all the lesbians he wished. He shook hands with Herb and Stacey, fussed over Ezra and Emma, then looked around the room for his parents, who apparently hadn't arrived. That was odd. He wondered if they were all right.

Maybe the DNR had raided his parents' home in the night and were waterboarding his father in some dingy basement. That would be ironic, his father having often stated that waterboarding was no big deal and he didn't see what the fuss was all about and if people didn't want to be waterboarded, then they should have kept better company and not lived in Afghanistan.

But where was his mother, and if his father was being water-boarded, why hadn't his mother phoned to tell him? Maybe they had her locked up, too. Maybe they didn't want any witnesses and had thrown her in a cell in solitary confinement and let her out only a half hour each day to exercise and she couldn't get word to Sam of their whereabouts, and by the time he found them, they were dead and buried in a pauper's grave on the prison grounds, deprived of a Christian burial. The DNR played hardball, that was for sure.

Then he heard someone say, "Hi, Sam," and it was his parents, who had woken up determined not to attend church, had eaten breakfast and gotten dressed, all the while declaring they would not attend meeting for worship, had gotten in their car and driven to Bruno's vowing never to darken the door of Hope Friends Meeting again, and had every intention of attending meeting one last time just to tell them so, then had entered Bruno's and there was Dan Woodrum greeting them and Ruby Hopper handing Gloria a baby twin, Gloria wasn't sure which one, and before they knew it, they had forgotten to be upset and were swept up in the general excitement. Quaker meeting for worship in an Italian restaurant! What would they think of next?

44

People milled about, then began staking out seats. Ruby Hopper had brought a music stand from home, which Sam placed next to the salad bar, beside the keyboard. He welcomed the congregation, updated them on the bat situation, admitted there was a bat killer in their meeting, perhaps right in their midst this very morning, so asked them to pray that the bat killer would confess and repent so this dark cloud could be lifted from their fellowship. A few people glanced in the direction of Charles Gardner, who stared resolutely forward. Sam paused, giving the killer ample opportunity to stand and confess, but no one did. This wasn't the movies, after all. It wasn't *Perry Mason*, where the killer leapt to his feet screaming, "I did it. I did it. I couldn't help it. They were driving me crazy. Getting in my hair and biting my neck. So I killed them. I killed the bats."

Instead, the bat killer was sitting in his living room across town, watching the Reverend Lester Hickam predict the end of the world, which would be any day now, since God was fed up with America for myriad reasons, chief among them letting Mexicans sneak into the country and take the best jobs, like roofing and picking fruit and working in slaughterhouses and cleaning toilets, perfectly good jobs that real Americans wanted to do but couldn't, since the Mexicans were already doing them.

"Boy, he's got that right," Leonard Fink said. "We've got to build ourselves a wall like the Chinese did. Don't get me wrong, I don't care for the Chinese, but they knew what they were doing when they built that wall."

He paused, contemplating the beauty of walls.

"I wished we lived closer to Brother Hickam's church," he said. "I hate that it's in Chattanooga and we're here. Sometimes I wonder if maybe we ought to move so we could join his church."

Had the people of Hope Friends Meeting heard Leonard say that, they would have happily rented a truck, helped them pack, and sent them on their way with their best wishes for a long and happy life in Chattanooga.

Back at Bruno's, the meeting for worship was progressing smoothly. Norma Withers had launched into their first song, "Amazing Grace." Their voices reverberated, bouncing off the hard surfaces—the tile floor, the brick walls, the pots and pans. Bruno wandered out from the kitchen, mesmerized by the music, joining them on the last verse, his rich tenor voice leading the way. Sam could scarcely believe it. Here was the man Sam had worried might kill him in order to steal Barbara away, now singing in their meeting for worship, not even having to look at the hymnal to see the words.

After singing, they began sharing their joys and concerns. Sam said what a joy it was to be meeting at Bruno's, and asked Bruno to stand so they could thank him, so he did and they did, clapping their gratitude. Then Sam's father stood and said how glad he was to be living in America, where people were innocent until proven guilty. Herb Maxwell rose to his feet and told about Stacey getting bit by their dog and how her hand was healing nicely, but that ongoing prayers would be appreciated. Chris and Kelly introduced their two visitors, one of whom was Chris's cousin, who was looking for a new church home. Chris satisfied any lingering curiosity when she said her cousin's name was Mary, and that the woman with her was Mary's wife, Beth.

Then Kelly stood and said the people at her job had volunteered to work at a food pantry in the inner city, and that the food pantry needed more helpers and would anyone be willing to join her and Chris the next Saturday morning at 8 a.m., when they passed out food to the families who lined up for help. Then and there, Barbara volunteered herself and Sam to help, even though Sam had planned to attend a pocketknife convention and had marked it on their refrigerator calendar three months before and Barbara had seen it, but had volunteered him anyway.

Hank Withers stood and talked about the delay in the meetinghouse addition because the bats in the trees were going at it hot and heavy, but not to worry because he was drafting a new plan, which would spare the trees while at the same creating a courtyard where they could hold outdoor services. Sam hated outdoor services. They were hot and buggy and the acoustics were bad. But he smiled anyway and thanked Hank for all he was doing.

Then Bruno came out from the behind kitchen counter. "I don't know if I'm allowed to speak since I'm not a member and I don't know anything about Quakers, but I just want to let you know that if any of you stay for dinner afterward, I'll give you a ten percent discount."

Wilson Roberts said amen, then reminded people that instead of having pie after church, they'd have tiramisu, compliments of the pie committee, who had approved paying Bruno twenty-five dollars a week for dessert for as long as they met at his restaurant. They had made the offer hoping Bruno would turn it down, which he hadn't done, at least yet, though they were praying he still might, since they only had a hundred dollars in the pie committee budget, which wouldn't last long at twenty-five bucks a week.

Sam thanked them for sharing their joys and concerns so readily, then prayed, asking God to provide so many volunteers for the food pantry they would have to turn helpers away. He hoped to be among those who were turned away, though he didn't say so out loud. He prayed for the bat killer, asking the Lord to bring him back into the fold of the Christian faith where he would be forgiven and restored. He prayed for the bats, for the parents and spouses and children of the dead bats, that in their hour of grief they would know God's comforting presence. He heard a few sniffs and a stifled sob in the congregation. Then they sang their second hymn, which was also "Amazing Grace," Norma Withers having forgotten, in the haze of Alzheimer's, that they'd already sung it, and everyone else being too embarrassed to remind her.

Then Sam preached about the sermons of Jesus and how many of them were given outdoors and if Jesus could worship outside, then they could worship in an Italian restaurant, even if it meant suffering hardships, such as giving up pie.

"We'll understand it better, by and by," he concluded, then sat down.

In the silence, they could hear Bruno puttering in the kitchen. It felt homey there in the restaurant, like they were children again and their mother was in the kitchen cooking dinner, and any minute would be calling out for them to wash their hands and come to the table. It made Sam think of his parents, which made him think of his father killing the bats. He had pretty much decided his father had done it. It was so like Charles Gardner, not because he was cruel, but because he was from a generation that took charge of things. If you had bats in your attic, you got rid of them. You didn't call the DNR to see if it was legal or ask permission from the church. You grabbed a two-by-four and started swinging, for crying out loud.

Yes, the more Sam thought about it, the more he thought it likely his father would spend the rest of his life in prison for slaughtering a hundred and seven bats. Worse yet, with his father in the pokey, sanding the floors at his parents' house would likely fall to him. If Bruno's hadn't smelled so good, Sam would have been utterly depressed.

45

The DNR lady didn't attend church, so while the Quakers of Hope Meeting were singing "Amazing Grace" for the third time that morning, she was sitting at her computer, writing a report about what was becoming known in the Department of Natural Resources as the Hope Meeting Massacre. She had spent the morning researching Quakerism, hoping to find a connection between their religion and animal abuse, but was coming up empty. Indeed, she was discovering just the opposite. Quakers tended to be peaceful and were one of the first organizations to support the humane treatment of animals. Nevertheless, it was a statistical probability that every group had at least one crackpot, and she was betting Hope Friends Meeting was no different.

She had narrowed her search to two people—Sam Gardner or his father, Charles. Or maybe even the both of them, a father-and-son killing team. Oh, how she hoped that was the case, and that she was the one to bust them. Her standing in the department had plummeted since she had ticketed the governor's brother for fishing without a license. But this would right the sinking ship that was her career.

She Googled both their names, and came up empty on Charles Gardner, but struck gold on Sam Gardner. There was only one reference, over three years old, but it was damning. Sam was prominently featured in a newspaper article on bigamy, when he had conducted the marriage of a man currently married to two other women. The reporter had scrounged up a copy of the marriage license with Sam's signature and had published it in the paper. Sam was quoted as saying it wasn't his fault, that no minister researched the marital status of the people they married, that being the responsibility of the county clerk who issued the license.

"Once a lawbreaker, always a lawbreaker," the DNR lady muttered. "I've got him now."

She consulted her notes from her encounters with Sam. He'd admitted to having too much to drink. A drinking pastor. That should have set off all kinds of alarms. His wife had said she'd been with him all day. What wife wouldn't lie to keep her husband out of jail? She was probably afraid of him. The poor thing. Married to a drunken pastor who probably knocked her around. And he had been so quick to point the finger at his own father. She saw that in her notes, too.

"Could your father have done this?"

"I'm not saying another word. Not one more word."

What kind of son would falsely accuse his own father to get out of trouble?

She glanced at her watch. She decided to swing by the meetinghouse to make sure they hadn't defied the no-entry order. It was a short drive, she was there within ten minutes, and to her surprise there wasn't a car in the parking lot. She had half expected to find them outside, armed with chainsaws, cutting down the bat trees and dancing naked around a fire like the savages they were.

With no one there, she decided to investigate the parsonage for clues. It's not like it was private property. It was owned by the church, after all. And wasn't everyone welcome in a church? Wasn't that the whole point of church, to throw open the doors and let people in?

The parsonage was unlocked. That was unusual. Most law-breakers assumed everyone else was as dishonest as they were so locked their doors. A tiny doubt tickled her mind. Maybe he was innocent. She dismissed the thought just as quickly. Any pastor who would aid and abet a bigamist, get drunk, slap his wife around, and try to frame his father had to be guilty. She went in. The inside of the parsonage was normal, with no indications of savagery. Well, of course there wouldn't be, she realized. There were church members in and out of the place. Sam would hide his sickness. He'd probably buried any evidence of his savagery.

She went outside, nosing around, starting in the front yard looking for irregular humps of earth. There were a few mole-hills, but nothing unusual. She made her way to the backyard, starting in the far corner, working her way toward the house. She stumbled over a slight mound of earth, then studied it more closely. It had recently been disturbed, more loosely packed than the dirt surrounding it. It was next to a redbud tree. Perhaps a family pet had been buried there. It looked like someplace a beloved member of the family would be buried, in the shade of a flowering tree.

She nudged the dirt with her foot, her curiosity growing. She hurried to her truck, retrieved a shovel, and began to dig, praying the Gardners wouldn't return while she was there. Digging down, she struck something solid. Well, almost solid. It gave a little bit. She dropped to her knees and began removing the dirt with her bare hands, uncovering a Tupperware bowl. This was certainly interesting. She lifted the bowl from the hole, opened it, and began retching. Whatever it was, and she couldn't tell what, had been brutally maimed. Then she realized it wasn't an it, it was a them. She began counting legs. Twenty-four legs. Six animals. They appeared to be bunnies. Bunnies! Chopped-up bunnies.

She'd seen a great deal in her years with the DNR, but nothing compared to this. Oh, she had heard of horrific cases, but they had happened in other places. She wished now she had gotten a search warrant. Sam would probably find a slick lawyer who'd have this evidence thrown out of court and get him off scot-free. Her first husband had been a lawyer. She despised lawyers. She wondered why no one ever chopped up lawyers. Bunnies? She couldn't believe it. Sam Gardner would pay. Even if he got away with this, she would get him back. She placed the bunnies back in the Tupperware bowl, buried them again, fussed over the area until it looked undisturbed, then committed its location to memory. She'd be back. This time with a search warrant.

46

~~

The tiramisu was delicious, even better than Ruby Hopper's Dutch apple pie, though no one said so. Meeting for worship had gone wonderfully. The change of location made everything feel fresh and new. People seemed genuinely pleased to be there, and lingered, eating dessert. A good number decided to stay for Sunday dinner, visiting among themselves until Bruno brought their meals. Herb Maxwell, being new to Quakerism and not realizing it was acceptable to drink wine in your home, alone, but never in public with other Quakers, ordered a glass of wine. Gloria Gardner stood next to Sam, watching him closely, ready to intervene should it prove necessary. She'd never realized it was such work being the mother of a boozehound.

As for Sam, he could hardly contain himself. It was the biggest crowd they'd had since he'd been there, if you included the customers who'd wandered in looking for something to eat, not realizing a church service was under way. But they were there, so it seemed only fitting to include them in the worship attendance. Of course they should be counted. Who was he to assume people hadn't come there to worship? Perhaps they had wakened that morning not realizing their need to worship and God had sent them to Bruno's, ostensibly for ravioli, but truth be known for more timeless fare. Why shouldn't Sam count them?

"Forty-five people," he whispered to Barbara. "Can you believe that? That's almost twice what we had last Sunday."

"Your father should have killed those bats a long time ago," she whispered back. Sam couldn't tell if she was joking. She had become more sarcastic lately. Sam was trying to be holy and nonjudgmental, so he moved away from his wife and went to talk with Ruby Hopper, who was visiting with Chris and Kelly and their friends, discussing the food pantry.

He introduced himself to Chris's cousin Mary, and her wife, Beth, who were on their second helping of tiramisu and seemed to be enjoying life in a Quaker meeting.

It felt odd having lesbians in the meeting. Sam supposed there had always been gays and lesbians in the meetings he'd pastored, they'd just never talked about it. He used to wish it were still that way, that gays and lesbians didn't feel the need to tell others who they loved. Then one day he realized he and Barbara announced who they loved every time someone saw them together, they just didn't have to say it out loud. Now he was of the mind that people saying who they loved was all right with him. It was better than people saying who they hated.

"Sam, it's so nice of you and Barbara to help at the food pantry next Saturday," Chris said.

"Yes, very nice," Kelly added.

"I think I'll join you," Ruby said. "If you still need help."

"Oh, I'm sure you'll be needed," Chris said. "We can't have too many helpers."

Kelly pulled a piece of paper from her purse and added Ruby's name. "You're number fifteen, Ruby. Can you believe that? We've had fifteen people volunteer to help just this morning. Your prayer worked, Sam."

Sam was amazed. They hadn't had fifteen people volunteer for anything in all the time he'd been there.

"The Maxwells are coming and bringing the babies," Chris said.

Ruby Hopper pointed to a man across the room, engaged in conversation with Wilson Roberts. "And there's a new attender who said he'd be happy to help. He didn't even know there was going to be church today. He was just walking by, saw all the people in here, came in for food, and ended up volunteering."

"That's wonderful," Sam said. "Maybe we'll have so many people volunteer, we really will have to start turning people away. Though I'd hate for that to happen. If someone really wanted to help, it'd be a shame to turn them down. Tell you what let's do, Chris. If you need to let go of someone, let go of me. That way no one's feelings will be hurt."

"That's very thoughtful of you, Sam," Chris said. "We'll keep that in mind."

"It's the least I can do," Sam said. He might make that pocketknife convention after all.

Wayne and Doreen Newby joined their group. "Wonder where the Finks are?" Wayne asked.

"They said they won't worship here because Bruno sells wine," Sam said.

"Boy, we would have served wine at our meetinghouse a long time ago if we'd known that," Wayne said.

Sam wanted to laugh, but knew he couldn't. Ministers had

to act as if each member's presence brought them immeasurable joy, and their absence deep sorrow.

"So why don't we just skip the building project, sell our meetinghouse, and meet here on Sundays," Doreen said. "This is nice."

"Where would we hold committee meetings?" Wayne asked.

"Who needs committee meetings?" Doreen said. "I'm tired of meetings anyway. They don't accomplish a thing."

It was hard to argue with that.

"But I suppose if we had to have a meeting, we could hold it at the parsonage," Doreen said. "We'd still own that."

Sam blanched. Church members in and out of his house every night, sitting in the living room, gabbing, bickering, poking around in his refrigerator for something to eat. Sam couldn't tell if Doreen was serious or not. She certainly sounded serious.

"That's a bit extreme," Ruby Hopper said. "We need our meetinghouse for funerals and weddings and—"

"We haven't had a wedding in years, and funerals could be held at the funeral home," Doreen said. "We could use the parsonage for everything else."

Sam was beginning to wish that whoever had killed the bats had driven over to Doreen's and knocked her around a bit.

47

Did you see the way everyone was avoiding me?" Charles Gardner said to Gloria on their way home from worship. "Oh, sure, everyone said hi, but after that they didn't want anything to do with me."

"You're just going to have to come right out and say you didn't do it."

"Nope, not going to do it. My character speaks for itself."

Old men were the worst, Gloria thought. They were so stubborn. Would it kill him to stand during the announcements and put everyone's doubts to rest? Just say he didn't kill the bats, and be done with it. People would believe him. He was the minister's father, for crying out loud. Of course they would believe him. But no, he had to be proud, had to act as if declaring his innocence were beneath him.

"I've got half a mind to turn in my membership and never go back," Charles said.

"You are not going to do that to our son. Think how that would make him feel, his own father quitting the church. You can't do that."

They rode in silence the rest of the way home. Charles settled in his recliner and was soon asleep. Gloria folded some laundry, then went online to look at bicycles. She'd been to Riggle's Hardware to buy another one, but Charley Riggle had promised Sam he wouldn't sell her another one. So she'd gone online to Amazon and had ordered a tandem bicycle so Charles could ride with her. He was spending all his time in his recliner, and getting fat, to boot. He could hardly bend down to tie his shoes. His belly lapped over his belt. She was going to whip him into shape if it killed her.

She'd been tracking the package. It was arriving by UPS the next day. She'd read the reviews people had written, noted that some of the reviewers mentioned having to assemble the bike, so had asked the man next door, who seemed to be a reasonably handy sort, if he minded doing that for her when the bike arrived. Not at all, he'd said. He'd be happy to help.

If she had asked Charles, it would never have gotten done.

The insurance company had settled quickly, hoping she wouldn't sue, writing her a check for a thousand dollars to buy a new bike, which had cost only five hundred dollars. So she bought two bicycle helmets, matching, and two sets of funny clothes she saw bicyclists wear, also matching. One for her, and one for Charles. They'd arrived the past Friday and she'd tried hers on while Charles was taking a nap. They were made of stretchy fabric, which she appreciated, even though it made her look like she was wearing sausage casings. She had a hundred and fifty dollars left over, so had bought a bicycle computer that clipped on the handlebars and showed how far she'd ridden and where she was and where she wanted to be. She was tired of getting lost and having to ask people for directions.

She'd be darned if she was going to spend the rest of her

life sitting on her butt staring at the TV, then having a stroke five years from now and drooling on herself in a nursing home until her heart gave out. Strangers mashing up her food and feeding it to her a spoonful at a time. Girl Scouts coming in at Christmastime to sing carols. Loud preachers coming in on Sunday afternoons, talking about the end of life and how nice heaven would be, and having to listen to them, because the aides would roll her wheelchair down to the community room whether she wanted to go or not. No sirree, Bob, not for her.

Charles would have a cow and refuse to go anywhere near the bicycle. He'd say she was ridiculous and there was no way he was going to cram himself into those bicycle clothes and climb on some stupid bike and ride around town so everyone could laugh at them.

She'd probably have to cry. It was the nuclear weapon of marriage, crying to get her way. She'd only done it twice. Once, when Richard Nixon had resigned and Charles had thought it was the end of all that was good and decent in America and had wanted to move to Canada. He'd started talking to Realtors and was a day away from putting their house on the market, when she let go with the tears. It'd taken three solid hours of crying before he came around. The second time was in 2007 when the New England Patriots had been caught spying on the New York Jets and hardly anything happened to them. They'd paid a little money, little for them, a slap on the wrist, and Charles Gardner ranted and raved and talked about moving to Norway, where people were honest. She thought it was just his usual ranting, until he signed up for an online class in Norwegian, and had applied for a visa. It took an entire day of crying then, off and on, every now and then breaking down into histrionic sobs. He'd finally caved in, late at night, and she'd made them eggs and toast for supper and he never mentioned it again, though she'd once found a magazine about Norway hidden under his side of the mattress.

But he'd flip out over riding a tandem bicycle with her. She could hear him now. "You're trying to get us both killed, is that it? You want us to end up in the hospital with all our bones broken, stuck in wheelchairs the rest of our lives? Is that what you want?"

What Gloria Gardner wanted was to have a life. She'd spent the past fifty years in the same small town, with the same people, doing the same thing day after day, the years grinding away, one after the other. She wanted to see new things, if only from a bicycle. Ride up and down unfamiliar streets looking at the houses, maybe eating somewhere they'd never eaten, maybe even riding to a nearby town. That was the only reason she'd moved to Hope, that and being closer to her sons and grandsons. The move hadn't quite met her expectations. Sam was always busy and the grandsons were gone, one in the army and one at college. Summers would be better. Barbara would be on vacation from school, and they would do things together. She liked Barbara, even felt sorry for her a little bit, having to put up with Sam. It wasn't that Sam was cruel or hateful, not at all, just that he was satisfied with so little, satisfied to stay close to home. Barbara would never see Paris, for that matter neither would she, them being married to Gardner men.

She pushed back from her computer and went downstairs. Charles was still asleep, but he'd be hungry when he woke up. They'd talk about what to eat for supper and settle for eggs and toast, their usual Sunday evening fare. She was pretty well fed up with eggs and toast, too.

48

When Lester Hickam finished preaching, a voice cut in over the organ music, inviting the faithful to join them in Chattanooga, at Lester Hickam's Evangelistic Center for a weeklong revival, whose purpose was to bring America back to God, but it cost money and they couldn't do it by themselves, so if people came to Chattanooga and made a love offering, God would bless them and return it tenfold.

Leonard Fink looked at Wanda and said, "We're going. Pack your bag."

A half hour later they were loading their Impala and on the road to save America.

They'd never been south of Louisville, so were nervous. Wanda began repeating the twenty-third Psalm, then moved on to the book of Revelation, which got them through Louisville and all the way to Nashville. Chattanooga was a downhill run from there, the traffic was light, and they were starting to relax.

The Finks had never been ones for vacations, a trip now and then to visit relatives in Illinois, a drive north to see the Amish in Shipshewana, but that was about it. To travel 450 miles in one day was unthinkable, unless one were saving America, then it was possible. They stopped for supper at a Big Boy, used the restroom, and were back on the road in an hour.

Neither one said anything about the bats, though they thought about them a great deal. Wanda wondered if Leonard might receive the death penalty for killing them. She didn't think so, but you couldn't be sure these days, what with Christians under attack and all. As for Leonard, he was thinking about his run for the school board and who he might get to head up his campaign. He was hoping to talk to Lester Hickam himself about it. Maybe Lester knew of someone who might help, him being close, personal friends with several governors and three candidates for the presidency. Surely one of them would see Leonard's potential and come to his aid.

"You don't think you'll be arrested for killing the bats, do you?" Wanda finally asked, thirty miles from Chattanooga.

"Not if they don't find out," Leonard said. "Besides, they were our bats, to do with as we pleased. God said so himself."

Wanda had been thinking about that. While God had given man dominion over the animals, that probably didn't include clubbing them with a two-by-four. She was beginning to think maybe Leonard shouldn't have done it, and that maybe the time had come for him to phone the DNR lady and tell her what he'd done. She had raised the subject with him the night before, but he had grown angry, telling her the only way to fight big government was to stop cooperating with it.

She was beginning to worry about Leonard. He'd always been mild-mannered, but after retiring had been watching news programs on television and had become disgruntled and paranoid. The year before, he'd bought a gun, certain the pres-

ident, who he knew for a fact didn't believe in God, was going
to outlaw them any day. They'd driven out in the country one
winter day, he'd rolled down the window and fired the gun
into a snowbank to see if it worked, which it did, nearly blow-
ing out their eardrums in the close confines of the car. Then
came the trips to Walmart to stock up on food and water that
he stored on shelves in their basement for when the monetary
system collapsed and you could buy food only if you had the
mark of the beast on your forehead.

Several times in the past few months, lying awake at night,
Wanda had worried that maybe something was wrong with
Leonard, that maybe some kind of disease had attacked his
brain and made him loopy. She had even suggested he make a
doctor's appointment for a physical, which had sent him into
a tirade against socialized medicine.

She was also starting to have her doubts about Lester
Hickam, not that she'd ever said so aloud. But in the thirty-
plus years they'd been listening to him, he'd predicted the return of Jesus on four separate occasions, and had been wrong
each time. She and Leonard had never discussed it, even
though the first time they'd sold their house and given their
things to nonbelievers, who would be sticking around and not
going to heaven.

One week, the month before, she had even caught herself
agreeing with something Sam said in a sermon. It was a strange
feeling, agreeing with her pastor, and she wasn't sure what to
make of it, but there it was—the realization that Sam might
have something to teach her. She'd tried shaking the feeling,
since dismissing him was so much easier, but the feeling persisted.

She'd begun doubting Lester Hickam after reading a mag-

azine article at the beauty shop she frequented about televangelists and their houses. For some reason, she had always
supposed Lester Hickam had lived in a 1950s ranch, just like
them. That was the thing about him, he seemed so much like
them, so ordinary, so down-to-earth. His wife Luella seemed
just as common. She didn't have the big hair and wear the
heavy makeup like the other televangelists' wives. She looked
like someone you'd see in Kroger checking a tomato for its
ripeness, someone you could walk right up to and chat with
about produce.

But there was a picture of their house in the magazine, with
a swimming pool and tennis courts and a gated entrance. That
was just their home in Chattanooga. They had a villa on the
beach in Hawaii, and a photographer had gotten close enough
to the Reverend Lester Hickam to take a picture of him rubbing suntan lotion on a woman's back and the woman didn't
look a thing like Luella. Wanda had never really gotten over
that. Every time she saw the reverend after that, it was all
she could think about, those hands touching another woman.
She'd mentioned it to Leonard and he'd blown up, screeching
about Photoshop and trick photography and how they could
make a picture of anyone doing anything these days. But she
was still pretty sure it was Lester Hickam with another
woman, certain enough that she had stopped sending Lester
Hickam the twenty dollars a month they'd sent for years.

49

The UPS man delivered Gloria Gardner's tandem bicycle at nine in the morning on Monday. Charles had taken to spending most of the morning in bed. That was another thing that drove Gloria crazy, Charles sleeping his life away. The neighbor man was home, and had the bike assembled and tuned up by lunchtime. Charles was still in bed, so the neighbor man and Gloria took it for a spin around the block. Gloria steered, while her neighbor supplied the muscle. He was pushing eighty, and didn't have much muscle to supply, but the street was level, the pavement smooth, and it was a pleasant spring day, so they rode another half hour, up and down the streets, past the school where Barbara worked, then pedaled by Riggle's Hardware and Drooger's Food Center. They turned the corner and headed toward home.

Charles was up when they arrived, and wondering why his wife was riding a tandem bicycle with a man she barely knew. This had been his one reservation about moving to the city, the depravity of it. He'd heard of it before, God-fearing people moving to the city from small towns and before long they were drinking in bars and starring in porno movies and riding tandem bicycles with complete strangers who'd slit their throats and toss them in a ditch somewhere. What in the world was Gloria thinking?

The neighbor seemed harmless, at least at first. He and Charles had chatted a few times and his wife had brought them over a casserole the day they moved in, but a lot of serial killers did that.

"My Lord, what are you wearing?" he asked Gloria.

"My bicycling outfit. Like it?" she asked.

"That's our bike?" he asked, changing the subject.

"You bet," she said. "Yours and mine. And we're going to ride it together, starting now. Whether you want to or not."

"I'm not getting on that thing."

"Charles Gardner, you're getting fat and boring. We are going to do something together, so get used to the idea."

"I'm always inviting you to watch TV with me," Charles said.

"Watching television is not doing something together. We're going to start bicycling together. It'll be good for us."

When they had first married, some fifty-odd years before, he'd had all kinds of energy. They'd hiked and camped and rode bicycles and played on the church softball team. After the boys came, they'd kept it up, then the boys left home and Charles Gardner hit the couch. He had been fifty years old and was married to the couch, except to attend antique tractor conventions.

She had hoped that buying an old house would get him moving, that he'd get up off the couch and start working. It had worked for a while, for six months or so, but now he was back on the couch.

In that moment, she realized he could never have killed the bats. It would have required work, sustained effort, and initiative. There was no possible way he could have done it. What had she been thinking?

"Charles Gardner, you will put on your bicycle clothes and your helmet, get on this bicycle, and go for a ride with me, or I'm never going to cook for you again."

"Bicycle clothes? What bicycle clothes?"

"The bicycle clothes I bought you to wear," Gloria said. "And the helmet, which you will wear. I don't want to spend the rest of my life visiting my brain-dead husband in a nursing home."

Charles groaned. "All I want is to be left alone to do what I want to do. Is that too much to ask?"

"Yes. Your bicycle clothes are in the bottom drawer of your chest. Your helmet is in the garage. We're leaving in fifteen minutes."

Despite his shortcomings, Charles Gardner had a few things going for him, one of them being his ability to realize when his wife meant business, so he went inside, peeled off his pajamas, took a quick shower, toweled off, stared at his fat in the bathroom mirror, then went into their bedroom, opened the bottom chest drawer, and was horrified to see a bright yellow shirt and black shorts, made of stretchy fabric, that would nevertheless require a winch to pull on. He struggled into the outfit, his fat lapping and bulging in pudgy bands. He dug around in his closet for a pair of tennis shoes, squeezed them on, checked himself in the mirror, and was pleased to see that some of his stomach fat had been pushed north to his chest. Maybe this wasn't such a bad idea after all.

He walked out to the garage, where Gloria was standing, his helmet in her hand.

"I rode a bicycle every day of my life until I was eighteen, and never once wore a helmet. I don't need one now."

"That's fine," Gloria said. "What did you plan on making us for dinner tonight?"

The helmet fit perfectly, as if she had measured his head while he'd been sleeping, which she had in fact done.

It had been thirty years since Charles Gardner was on a bicycle, but he took to it quickly, and even began enjoying it, though he didn't say so. Gloria steered, while Charles pedaled from the back, shouting instructions. They bickered the first several blocks, then began to relax, finding a proper cadence, weaving in and out of the neighborhood streets.

"Let's go by and show Sam," Charles yelled out from the backseat.

Five minutes later, they turned down the meetinghouse lane and were pulling into the meeting's parking lot noticing a half-dozen DNR trucks and cars parked in the parsonage driveway. Sam was standing on the sidewalk, surrounded by a group of officers. While Sam had never been deeply tanned, he was paler than usual.

The DNR lady, Gloria recognized her from the week before, was waving a sheet of paper in Sam's face.

"This is a warrant to search your yard," she said, pushing Sam aside.

"Hold on there," said Charles Gardner, who had not missed an episode of *Law & Order* since 1990. "Let me see that warrant."

He studied the warrant carefully. "This warrant's no good. Sam doesn't own this property. It belongs to the church, but the church isn't listed as the property owner. And it doesn't say what you're searching for."

He wasn't sure any of that actually mattered, but it sounded terribly official and gave the DNR lady pause.

"What are you looking for?" Charles persisted.

"Animal or human remains," the DNR lady snapped.

"People have been living in this house almost thirty years. Of course you're going to find animal remains. Where else do people bury their pets?"

"We're not looking for pets. We're looking for something else."

"So you're just going to dig up the churchyard without telling us what you're looking for? Did I wake up this morning in Russia? I don't think so." Charles had heard that line on television years before and had wanted to use it ever since.

The DNR lady glared at him. At times like this, she wished the department had given her a Taser. She had asked for one several times, without success.

"We're coming back, and when we do, we're going to dig up this entire yard. He's hiding something," she said, pointing to Sam, "and we're going to find it."

50

Whose bike is that?" Sam asked, after the DNR lady and her minions had left.

"It's ours," his mother said.

"Why are you wearing those funny clothes?"

"It was your mother's idea," Charles said.

"I thought you weren't going to ride anymore after your accident," Sam said to his mother.

"I made no such promise."

Sam sighed.

"Why does the DNR want to dig up your yard?" Gloria asked.

"They obviously think I've hidden something there."

"Have you?" Charles asked.

"Of course not. I haven't even lived here that long. Do they think I've been killing people and burying them in my yard? That woman is crazy."

"Maybe they think you killed the bats," Charles said. "And that if you killed the bats, maybe you've been killing other things."

"I've never killed a bat in my entire life," Sam protested. "I thought maybe you killed them."

"I wouldn't do that," Charles said with great indignation. "Why would you even think that?"

"Because you said you would and you killed those snakes that one time, and the nest of mice," Sam reminded him. "You didn't think I knew about the mice, did you?"

"Who told you?"

"Mom."

"I told you not to tell him I told you," Gloria said to Sam.

"Oops," Sam said. "Sorry."

"It doesn't matter," Charles said. "Everyone kills snakes and mice."

"So did you kill the bats, too?" Sam asked his father.

"No, he didn't kill the bats," Gloria Gardner said. "I thought at first maybe he had, but then it occurred to me he was too lazy to do something like that. It would have been too much work."

Charles listened, wondering whether or not to be offended.

"So what will they find when they dig up your yard?" Charles asked. "You got anything to hide? Old *Playboy* magazines you didn't want Barbara to find? Whiskey bottles you didn't want to set out in the trash for the neighbors to see?"

"Nothing. I've got nothing to hide. I've not done anything."

Then he remembered the bunnies.

"Well, I've maybe done one thing, but it was an accident. I didn't do it on purpose."

"What did you do?" Gloria said, dreading the answer. Sam had always seemed a little off to her. Maybe a little too much of a moral stickler, a little too eager to please. Those were the kind of people with secrets.

"I killed a bunch of bunnies," Sam said.

"My gosh, that's sick," Gloria said. "Why would you do that?"

"It was an accident. They were in a nest in some high grass and I mowed right over them. It was terrible. Fur and bones and blood shooting out the side of the mower." He shook with disgust at the memory of it.

"What's that got to do with your yard?" Charles asked.

"I buried them in a Tupperware container next to the red-bud tree."

They stood there, silently contemplating the trouble it would cause if the DNR lady unearthed a Tupperware bowl of baby rabbits that appeared to have died at the hands of a sadistic lunatic.

"We better get those rabbits before they do," Charles Gardner said. "Do you have a shovel?"

Sam hustled to the garage, grabbed a shovel, and led his parents to the slight mound beside the redbud tree. He began digging. The earth was loose and before long Sam's shovel made a soft thump, and he dropped to his knees and began to clear away the dirt with his hands, exposing the Tupperware bowl.

"That's Barbara's salad bowl," Gloria Gardner said. "She called me last week wanting to know if I had it."

"Please don't tell her, or I'm in real trouble," Sam said.

He lifted the bowl from the tomb, set it aside, and began filling in the hole, topping it off with dirt from the flower bed, then scattering leaves atop it so it would appear undisturbed.

"Have you buried anything more in the yard?" Charles Gardner asked. "Any orphans, or hobos, or homeless people?"

"Charles, that's disgusting. Sam wouldn't do that." Gloria looked at Sam. "You wouldn't do that, would you?"

"Of course not. It was just the rabbits, and it was an accident."

"What are we going to do with them?" Sam's father asked.

"We can't leave them here, that's for sure," Sam said. "That DNR lady would sniff them right out."

"Give them to me," Gloria Gardner said.

Sam handed the bowl of rabbits to his mother.

"What are you going to do with them?" he asked.

"It's better you don't know," she said. "You'll need deniability."

There was a basket on the front of their bike. She had ordered it knowing it would come in handy, though she never imagined using it to dispose of evidence from a crime scene. She reminded Sam to wipe his fingerprints from the shovel and Tupperware, yet again grateful she had watched so many crime shows, then placed the Tupperware bowl in the basket, told Charles it was time to go, and pedaled away.

They turned right at the end of the meetinghouse lane and headed toward Main Street, taking the backstreets, ending up in back of Bruno's, pulling alongside his dumpster, where she pried the lid from the bowl, shook out the bunnies, who, as a testament to Tupperware, were amazingly well-preserved in spite of their circumstances.

"If anyone smells them, they'll just think it's the regular dumpster smell," she explained to Charles, who was duly impressed by his wife's ingenuity.

She placed the empty bowl back in her basket.

"Throw that in there, too," he said.

"A perfectly good Tupperware bowl? Not on your life."

They pedaled home, meditating on the unshakable bond between parents and their children and how a parent's work was never really done.

51

~~

H ank Withers, Wayne Newby, and Wilson Roberts were gathered in Hank's basement, seated around a poker table, the blueprints for the new meetinghouse addition spread out in front of them.

"If this is a trustee meeting, why aren't Leonard, Dan, and Sam here?" Wilson Roberts asked Hank. "They should be here, too."

"Because Leonard's a stick-in-the-mud, and Sam and Dan can't know anything about this. It's too risky for them," Hank said. "They have their careers to think of."

"What's too risky for them?" Wayne asked.

"What I'm about to propose," Hank said.

He had phoned them the night before, asking them to come to his house the next day at one o'clock, during Norma's naptime.

"Let's hear it," Wilson said.

Hank liked that about Wilson. Cut to the chase. No dilly-dallying. All business.

"These stupid bats are killing us," Hank said. "I've been racking my brain trying to think of a way to build around these trees, and there's no way to do it, unless we go straight up, which we're not going to do."

"Yesterday at meeting you said you were working on a way to build around the trees and make a courtyard," Wayne said. "What happened to that plan?"

"It's impossible," Hank said. "I'd have to squeeze a hallway down to four feet wide and code requires at least six feet. Unless, of course, they let us remove one tree, but they won't, so it's beside the point."

"How do you know they won't?" Wilson asked.

"I phoned the county planning this morning. They said the DNR only allows exemptions for buildings vital to public welfare, and even then we'd have to purchase suitable habitat elsewhere and relocate the threatened species. All at our own expense."

Wilson and Wayne absorbed the news.

"So if we'd cut down the trees this last week, we'd have been free and clear," Wayne said.

"That's right," Hank said. "There's nothing they could have done to us. In fact, if we had cut those trees down even a half hour before that DNR lady came out and stopped our building, we'd have been free and clear. Now if something is wrong, it's wrong all the time. Take murder. If I murder someone, then it's wrong whether I do it now or a half hour from now. So how can cutting down a tree be perfectly fine one moment, but thirty minutes later be wrong?"

Hank looked across the table at them, studying their faces.

"Doesn't make any sense to me," Wilson said.

"Men, we've got a job to do," Hank said. "I won't lie, it could get us in serious trouble, but it has to be done if the Lord's work is to move forward."

Hank Withers had never seemed all that concerned about the Lord's work until Olive Charles had kicked the bucket and left them a million dollars to spend.

"What do you have in mind?" Wayne asked.

"What I'm about to tell you goes no further than this group. You can't tell Sam, Leonard, or Dan. You can't tell anyone ever. You can't admit to anything, no matter what pressure is brought to bear. Do I have your word?"

Wayne and Wilson nodded their agreement.

"We're going to cut down those trees," Hank said. "Tonight. At seven o'clock. There's a Christian education committee meeting tonight at Wayne's house. Sam and Barbara will be there, and Norma and Doreen will be there. I've asked Sam and Barbara to come by and pick up Norma at six forty-five. No one will be anywhere near the meetinghouse."

"That's right, I remember Doreen telling me we had to eat supper early tonight and I had to make myself scarce," Wayne said.

Hank reached into his back pocket, pulled out a map of the churchyard trees, and placed it on the table, smoothing it out.

"These two trees have to come out," Hank said, plucking a pencil from behind his ear and pointing at the offending trees. "They're mostly dead anyway. We had had them slated for removal this fall. So we're going to hurry the process along. With these two trees gone, we can get our addition built."

"What about the bats?" Wilson asked.

"They'll be out of there by seven," Hank assured them. "The sun is starting to set and most all of them have left the trees by six fifty. I've been over there the past three evenings watching."

"Where will they go if we cut down their trees?" Wilson asked.

"They'll find someplace else to hang upside down and forni-cate," Wayne said. "What do we care? It's not like there aren't more trees. Geez, we own ten acres of trees."

It hadn't escaped Hank's notice that Wilson and Wayne were using the word *we*.

"Men, we can't afford any mistakes. Here's how we're going to do it. We meet at six forty-five, at the Panera on Washing-ton Street."

"The one on the back side of our property?" Wilson asked.

"Yes, that's the place," Hank said. "I'll bring the chainsaw. We go behind Panera, enter our property from the east, cut through the woods, take down the trees, and get out. The whole thing shouldn't take fifteen minutes. Twenty, at the most."

"Can we have supper at Panera afterward?" Wilson asked. "I'll be hungry after all that work."

"No," Hank said. "In and out. Like ghosts."

"He could go to Panera before we cut down the trees," Wayne pointed out. "Just so long as he was ready to go by six forty-five."

"I love their chicken chipotle sandwich," Wilson said. "I could eat one every day."

"Their soup's good, too," Wayne said. "And Doreen really likes their applewood chicken salad."

"Focus, men," Hank demanded. "We're not here to talk about the menu at Panera. Now let's go over it again. What time are we meeting?"

"Six forty-five," they said in unison.

"Good. Not a minute earlier, not a minute later."

Hank ran through the plan again, then Wilson and Wayne left, before Norma woke from her nap.

52

Sam sat on their screened-in porch, watching the birds at the feeder. It was his favorite room, it looked out into the backyard, into the woods, and the little creek that marked the west side of the meeting's property. If he were arrested for bat killing, he would certainly miss sitting here. He liked coming out here at night, when he couldn't sleep. Over the trees, he could see the haze of lights from the city, but it seemed far away.

He felt bad for the bats, and had racked his brains trying to figure out who would squish a hundred and seven Indiana bats to death. Some low-life scum. He thought it had to be someone in the meeting, someone who had a key to the place. Then he remembered he forgot and left the meetinghouse unlocked half the time, so it could have been any low-life scum.

He had been so certain it was his father, he hadn't given much thought to who else it might have been. Not that his father was low-life scum. He just wasn't one to let a few rules get in his way if something needed doing.

Sam thought back over that day. He'd had oatmeal for

breakfast, along with three pieces of bacon and a glass of orange juice. He and Barbara had read the morning paper on the screened-in porch, and she'd left for work. He'd washed the breakfast dishes, taken a bath, gotten dressed, then looked out the window to see several trucks and cars pull down the meetinghouse lawn. They had snooped around, found bats in the meetinghouse attic, then decreed the meetinghouse off-limits.

He remembered all that perfectly well. Then what? He racked his brain, trying to recall what else had happened. Oh, yeah, he had phoned Ruby Hopper to tell her about the meetinghouse being closed. Had he phoned anyone else that morning? Yes, he remembered talking to someone. He clicked on his cell phone and began scrolling through the list of calls made, flipping back to that date, and there, just after Ruby Hopper, was the name Wilson Roberts.

He remembered that now. Wilson Roberts. He pictured the portly, arthritic man squeezing through the attic access, chasing down all those bats on his bad knees, and bludgeoning them. He couldn't see it. Maybe at one time, Wilson could have fit through the attic access, but that had been a lot of pies ago. No, it couldn't have been Wilson.

Maybe a woman did it. Why did everyone automatically assume it was a man? He Googled the phrase *women serial killers* and came up with an extensive list of possibilities. So much for the fairer sex. He began writing down all the women who knew about the bats. Ruby Hopper, Barbara, and his mother. He ruled out Barbara. She'd been at work, and when she wasn't there she'd been with him. He didn't think his mother would do it. Maybe if his father were found murdered, he'd suspect his mother, but not bats. She'd always liked animals. He tried to recall everything he knew about Ruby Hopper. Hadn't she once mentioned growing up on a farm? That was interesting. Farm women had a no-nonsense air about them, and thought nothing of killing chickens and pigs and cows. He could maybe see Ruby Hopper picking up a cleaver and dispensing with a colony of bats. But she wasn't an idiot. She wouldn't have put the bats in a trash bag and tossed it at the end of the meeting-house lane for the trash man to pick up. Only a moron would do that, and Ruby Hopper was no moron.

So Sam thought of all the morons in the meeting. That narrowed the list of suspects down to two—Leonard and Wanda Fink. Plus, Leonard was skinny and could slip through the attic access like the snake he was. And they had a key to the meetinghouse and were constantly over there, nosing around, looking through Sam's files. Yes, he'd known that. They hadn't even bothered to put them back in order, the idiots.

At the moment Sam was thinking of them, Leonard and Wanda were in their third day of Lester Hickam's weeklong revival, which so far had set them back a thousand dollars, money they didn't have to spend, though Leonard had told Wanda that was a cheap price to pay to save America. Lester Hickam was passing the hat on the hour, every hour, men in suits circulating KFC buckets up and down the rows while Lester and Luella wept onstage. You couldn't help but want to give them money. Lester would read aloud the names of the givers, his hand raised in the air, with Luella beside him, praising the Lord. If Luella knew about the women Lester was rubbing suntan oil on, it hadn't appeared to bother her.

Leonard hadn't yet been able to get Lester Hickam alone to seek counsel on his run for the school board. There were obvious obstacles to Leonard's run, the chief one being Leonard's dropping out of high school when he was seventeen, but he wasn't one to let minor details discourage him. Wanda wasn't quite sure she wanted to be married to a politician. There were too many temptations for men in politics, too many women throwing themselves at them. There was something about power that some women couldn't resist. She prayed Leonard could withstand them. Leonard hadn't given any indication of unfaithfulness. He wasn't the kind of man to excite the imaginations of women, but one never knew.

Wanda was starting to wish they'd never come to Lester Hickam's revival. The first day or two had been interesting, getting to see in person what she had seen only on television. Even though she had her doubts about Lester Hickam, he did know how to work a crowd. She had to give him that. And he had a Bible verse for everything. He'd even spoken briefly about the magazine article. It was Satan's attack, there was not a shred of truth in it. The mansion at the beach wasn't theirs. It belonged to one of the church members who had made it available to Lester and Luella in order to refresh their spirits after the rigors of ministry. Yes, he'd rubbed lotion on a young lady, but she had been in a dreadful accident, had lost both her hands, and had asked for Lester's help. It was true you couldn't see her hands in the photograph. Luella said how grateful she was to have such a kind husband who would help handless women, but if you watched her close, when the cameras weren't rolling, she didn't seem all that grateful.

By the third day, Wanda was ready to head home, but Leonard said as long as they were in Chattanooga, it would be a shame not to go see Dollywood in Pigeon Forge, which was only a few hours away, over the mountains. The vacation season hadn't started and a cabin was available with picturesque views of the world-famous Smoky Mountains, with all the comforts of home. Or so said the brochure they found at the rest stop on Interstate 40. But when they checked in and went to their cabin, it smelled like mildew on account of the hot tub, which Wanda used to wash their clothes.

Leonard left the cabin to gas up the car, so Wanda phoned Norma Withers, who told her the Department of Natural Resources was searching for the bat killer and pushing for the death penalty. Wanda wasn't sure what part of that was true and what part was the Alzheimer's; one never knew with Norma.

"Who do they think did it?" she asked Norma.

"That minister of ours," Norma said. "What's his name? Stan?"

Stan had been their minister two ministers before; they all kind of blurred together after a while.

They chatted a bit longer. Norma told her about trying to eat at Bruno's, but the rudest man kept talking and made her play the piano even though all she wanted to do was eat her ravioli. Then she mentioned seeing some old people riding past her house on a bicycle built for two, and that's when Wanda realized nothing Norma had said could possibly be true.

53

It was six thirty and Sam Gardner was washing the supper dishes. With a meeting to attend, it had been a quick meal, grilled cheese and tomato soup. He was dreading the meeting, having been roped into attending by his wife, who'd gotten wind that Doreen Newby wanted the adult Sunday school class to study a book by a fascist kook who had his own television show and had written a book about Jesus, which had made the bestsellers list, thoroughly depressing Sam.

"There's no way on God's green earth I'm going to read a book written by that gasbag. We're finally getting some nice young couples in the meeting, and we're going to scare them off with nonsense like that," Barbara had told Sam. "So I need you to come to the CE meeting and back me up."

What was it with Doreen Newby anyway? All Sam wanted was to lie in his hammock after working all day and maybe read a good book or go for a walk. But no, he had to attend yet another meeting to keep someone from doing something stupid and killing the church.

He was drying the last dish when their kitchen phone rang.

Their personal calls came on their cell phones, so it was either someone selling something or someone wanting something.

He picked up the phone and said hello.

"Is this the pastor?"

"Yes, this is Sam Gardner. I'm the pastor of Hope Friends Meeting. Who is this?"

"My name's Bob Rush, and I was wondering if you could maybe help me."

Sam knew the spiel by heart. Bob's mother was in Arkansas, dying, and he needed money to be with her before she passed away, so if he came by the church, could Sam give him gas money?

"I won't give you cash," Sam said. "But if you want, I can meet you at the gas station and tank up your car."

At that point, they usually started arguing with Sam that they preferred cash, that they already had gas in their car, and needed the money for food. Sam would offer to meet them at the grocery store and buy them food, which made them mad, and they would continue arguing with Sam, who wouldn't budge, then they would tell him he was no kind of Christian and hang up. He'd been through it countless times.

But Bob Rush surprised him. "I'd appreciate that. I'm at the Shell station on Washington Street. I'm driving a gray Corolla."

"I can be there in fifteen minutes," Sam said.

"See you then, and thank you very much."

It was maybe a scam, but at least it was a polite scam, which Sam appreciated. He appreciated it all the more when he realized it would get him out of attending the Christian education meeting.

"I can't go to the meeting," he told Barbara. "I just got a call from someone who needs help. Don't forget to pick up Norma Withers on your way to the Newbys' house."

"If we end up studying that stupid book and it causes everyone with half a brain to quit our church, it's your fault," she said before leaving.

Sam drove to the Shell station, passing Panera Bread, where he saw Hank, Wayne, and Wilson standing in the parking lot, next to Hank's car.

He liked Panera and wondered why they hadn't invited him.

He pulled into the Shell station, found Bob Rush, filled his car with gas, shook his hand, said he was sorry about his mother, and wished him Godspeed.

He walked back to his car, and noticed Hank, Wayne, and Wilson walking across the field behind Panera toward the meetinghouse property. Hank was carrying a chainsaw.

That's when it occurred to him that Hank, Wayne, and Wilson were on the trustees' committee and were probably clearing brush on the back side of the meetinghouse property. He had to hand it to the trustees, they certainly kept up on things. They had the prettiest churchyard in all of Hope. It gave Sam a good feeling, knowing the people in his meeting were hard at work for the betterment of God's creation.

Feeling good about the world, he decided to celebrate by visiting the Dairy Queen, where he ate an ice cream cone dipped in crunchies, then swung by his brother Roger's house, where he spent a half hour viewing the improvements his brother and fiancée had made to their home, reminded them he was available to perform their wedding should they decide to set a date, then went home, his work done.

54

⌒

If Wilson Roberts had once enjoyed a carefree childhood, playing in the woods, those days had long since passed. By the time he and Wayne and Hank had walked fifty yards across the field behind Panera and entered the meetinghouse property on its eastern edge, he was covered with sweat and panting heavily.

"My gosh, Wilson, you look like death," Hank said. "Don't you ever exercise?"

"Not if I can help it."

Wayne Newby wasn't faring any better. In the first twenty yards, he had twisted his ankle and required Hank's assistance to go farther.

"You two are pathetic," Hank said, propping Wayne up. "I'm older than both of you."

"Yeah, well, maybe if I'd had a cushy job sitting on my butt drawing pictures of houses, my knees wouldn't be shot, but I actually had to get up off my duff and work for a living," Wayne said.

Besides lugging Wayne, Hank also carried a chainsaw and

gas can. He held out the chainsaw to Wilson. "Wilson, can you carry the chainsaw?"

"I don't possibly see how," Wilson said.

Hank was trying hard to remember why he had asked for Wayne and Wilson's help.

"You two wait here. I'll do this myself."

"I need an ambulance," Wayne said. "I don't think I can make it back to my car."

Hank muttered something, they couldn't tell what, and struck off through the woods, a lone pioneer, fighting the heartless bureaucracy that would deny them their church addition.

"I hope the trees don't fall on the meetinghouse," Wayne said. "Do you think he knows what he's doing?"

"Sure, he served on the limb committee all those years," Wilson pointed out. "He's great with a chainsaw."

They heard the chainsaw fire up, like angry bees, rising and falling in pitch as Hank cut his way through the first tree. Several minutes later, they heard a creak and a dull thud as the tree hit the ground.

"That was pretty quick," Wayne said.

"Maybe we ought to get back to the cars," Wilson said. "Hank can catch up with us."

They started back through the field, Wayne leaning on Wilson.

Hank began cutting down the second tree. The first tree, mostly rotten, and the smaller of the two, had been a whiz. He'd dropped it not ten feet from the meetinghouse, right where he'd planned. The second tree took a bit longer, but dropped neatly into place, and after that, he was home free, disappearing back into the woods toward Wayne and Wilson, who were now halfway across the field, hobbling toward their cars. He caught up with them at the edge of the parking lot.

"We're good to go," he told them. "No one saw me. In and out, just like we planned."

"You don't think they'll know it was us?" Wayne asked.

"Not if we don't talk. That means you can't tell your wife," Hank said. "You can't tell anyone. As far we're concerned, this never happened."

"Never happened," Wilson repeated. "Got it. Lips are zipped."

"Doreen told me not to come home until eight thirty," Wayne said, glancing at his watch. "Want to get a sandwich at Panera?"

Hank declined, but Wilson, a bachelor, thought that sounded wonderful. They ordered, picked up their food, and settled into a booth.

"You know, I've been thinking," Wayne said. "You and I really didn't do anything. We didn't cut down the trees. Heck, we barely even went on the meetinghouse property, but now we're just as guilty as Hank, and he's the one who did everything. It was his idea, his chainsaw, his gas, he's the one who cut the trees. But you and I are going to be in just as much trouble if he gets caught."

Wilson thought about that. "That doesn't seem right, does it?"

"Not to me it doesn't. Do you think maybe he brought us along so he could pin it on us?"

"I don't think Hank would do that," Wilson said. "Maybe he thought he'd need our help."

"Yeah, you're probably right. I sure hope this doesn't come back to haunt us."

"I don't see that it could," Wilson said. "The only people who know what happened are us, and we're sure not going to tell. I'd say we're free and clear."

55

It was a perfect night, as far as Sam was concerned. He stretched out on the hammock on their screened-in porch and read a book until he dozed off. It was a murder mystery, chock-full of blood and gore. The book was open against his chest, when Barbara nudged him awake.

"I don't know why you read that trash," she said. "There's all kinds of wonderful literature available, and you fill your mind with that garbage."

"I read it because I can," Sam said. "It's a free country. I can read whatever I wish. When you stop and think about it, I'm defending the freedom of the press. You might want to think about that, little Miss Librarian."

"Well, you're going to get to read some more garbage. The CE committee decided to let Doreen have her way. So now we'll be reading that god-awful book for Sunday school."

"Not me," Sam said. "I'm boycotting the class. That's a dreadful book and I'm not wasting my money on it. Instead, I will be offering an alternative Sunday school class where we will study seditious literature penned by heretics. Would you like to be in my new class?"

"I most certainly would. Why don't you scoot over and we'll talk about it some more."

There was something about church committee meetings that put Barbara in a mood to snuggle, and though Sam had never understood how spending the evening with a group of Quakers could ramp up one's hormones, he wasn't about to argue. He scooched over to make room for Barbara. They talked about the committee meeting, Barbara vented a bit, Sam mentioned seeing the trustees and visiting his brother, Roger, and his fiancée, Christina. He mentioned that the DNR lady had come by earlier in the day wanting to dig up the yard and look for bodies. He didn't mention the bunnies, worried it might dampen her desire to snuggle.

Hammocks are wonderful for reading and naps, but awkward for other pursuits. They tried their best and were ultimately successful. Afterward, they showered, went to bed, and promptly fell asleep.

When Sam woke up the next morning, Barbara had left for work. He felt rested and alert. He jumped out of bed, pulled on shorts and a shirt, ate his morning oatmeal, and had just set up his computer at the kitchen table to start his day's work, when he heard a truck pull down the meetinghouse lane.

It was the DNR lady, back with shovels and a search warrant, and two strong men to help with the digging.

Sam met them in the driveway. He thought about calling his father, who had performed so admirably the day before, then decided against it, thinking it might be wiser to cooperate. After all, he had nothing to hide, having disposed of the bunnies.

"You can look for anything you want," he said. "Just please put the dirt back in the holes when you're done."

Without hesitation, the DNR lady marched to the redbud tree and began digging exactly where the bunnies had been.

Sam thought that was odd. How had she known to dig there? It was like she had dug there before.

She dug down one foot, then two feet, then frowned, moved over a bit and began digging again. They worked their way around the tree while Sam watched from the screened-in porch. The DNR lady was perplexed, then agitated, and began digging deeper, flinging shovelfuls of dirt behind her.

Sam walked outside to the redbud tree.

"Perhaps if you tell me what you're looking for, I can help you," he said.

"You know what I'm looking for. They were here this past Sunday."

Sam had to be careful. He didn't want to lie, but neither did he want to spend the rest of his life in jail when he'd done nothing wrong.

"What was here this past Sunday?" Sam asked.

She didn't answer. He had her dead to rights. She couldn't very well admit to seeing a Tupperware bowl of diced rabbits, discovered under dubious circumstances.

She began walking around the yard, looking for possible graves, every now and then probing with a long metal rod or digging a hole. One of the men retrieved a metal detector from the truck and began walking back and forth across the yard. He unearthed several coins, a rusty beer can, and a garden trowel Barbara had inadvertently covered with mulch the month before.

"You've made my wife's day," Sam said, wiping off the tool. "She's been looking for this. It's her favorite trowel."

He texted Barbara. Found your trowel.

"I know you killed those bats," the DNR lady said. "I know you torture animals. You're not fooling me."

"I've told you several times I didn't do anything to the bats. I wouldn't do that. I want to find out who did it just as much as you do," Sam said.

She snorted in disbelief, then turned to the two men. "While we're here, we might as well check on the bats in the trees. Let's go."

They stowed their tools in the truck, retrieved a ladder, and walked across the parking lot toward the meetinghouse. Sam followed behind them, hoping to see the bats himself.

It turned out the ladder wasn't needed. The trees were flat on the ground, the rotted trunks broken apart by the force of their fall. The DNR lady didn't speak for the longest time. She walked around the trees, occasionally hauling off and kicking the trunk, then inspected the hollowed sections where the bats once lived. She opened her mouth several times to speak, but nothing came out.

"I don't know anything about this," Sam said. "This is the first time I've seen it. I didn't do it."

Sam was grateful the DNR lady had put her shovel back in the truck, otherwise she'd probably have beaten him to death.

"When did this happen?" she demanded.

"I have no idea."

"What is with you people? You wipe out nearly an entire colony of bats, then cut down the trees where they lived."

"There's no proof any of the church members did any of this," Sam said, though it was unlikely Episcopalians on a rampage had broken into a Quaker meeting to club bats.

"Don't be an idiot. If it wasn't you, it had to be someone in your church."

"I can't imagine who would do this," Sam said.

For someone who had been to college and had a master's degree, Sam Gardner could be slow to arrive at conclusions glaringly obvious to everyone else.

He recalled seeing the trustees the night before. But they were working on the back side of their property. If they had wanted to cut down the trees, they would have come down the lane, parked in the meetinghouse parking lot, and cut down the trees. They wouldn't have parked at Panera, and walked through a field carrying a chainsaw and gas can. Would they? They would have parked at the meetinghouse. Wouldn't they? Unless they didn't want to be seen by anyone who knew them. Is that why he and Barbara had been asked to pick up Norma? To get them out of the way?

Hank Withers wouldn't do that, would he? Wayne Newby might. Any man who would hide a girlie magazine from his wife would stoop to anything. But Hank Withers? Sam didn't think so. He wondered about Wilson Roberts. He couldn't see Wilson Roberts making this kind of effort unless there was pie involved. But given the right inducements, he might do it.

The DNR lady was staring at him. "You know who did this, don't you? I can see it in your face."

"If I did suspect someone, I certainly wouldn't tell you," he said. "At least not until I talked with them."

"Then you better talk with them, and quick, because I want some names. You got that, buster?"

Sam nodded, sobered by the realization that he might well be the pastor of a heartless gang of felons.

56

Sam tried for several hours to write his sermon, but was too distracted to concentrate. Several weeks before, he had begun a new series on church history, hoping to avoid controversy, had worked his way up to the Council of Jerusalem in AD 50, where the apostles gathered to discuss whether new members had to have the tips of their wieners whacked off in order to join the church. He had begun the series hoping to avoid the topic of sex, was only on the third sermon, and was already talking about wieners. Sex, sex, sex, it was all the church ever thought about.

Sam was already tired of the series. He'd covered twenty years in three sermons, and had nearly two thousand years to cover, or another three hundred sermons, as near as he could figure. He wondered whether people would notice if he abandoned the series. Maybe he could preach on the care of God's creation and how just because God gave humans authority over the animals and trees, it didn't mean they could do whatever they wanted to them. He leaned back in his chair and thought of that—a robust sermon that would make the guilty party, or parties, feel such shame they would come forward and confess their sins and go to jail, where they would get right with the Lord and write a book about the experience, which Sunday school classes all over the country would read, and the royalties would be donated to the meeting to fund a raise for Sam in appreciation for preaching the sermon that had set the guilty party on the straight and narrow road to life.

It was probably too much to hope for.

He thought it best to let the sermon season, so decided to visit Hank Withers under the guise of checking on Norma and her Alzheimer's. Perhaps Hank might let something slip. They lived very near the meeting, so Sam rode his bicycle, winding his way through the streets and arriving at the Witherses' home, a boxy place with peculiar angles and lots of glass, the kind of house an architect would live in.

Hank answered the door and invited Sam in. Norma was in their kitchen and offered Sam iced tea, which he gladly accepted. Hank ushered him to a chair at the kitchen table, Norma brought him his tea, and Hank said, "What brings you to our home today?"

"Oh, nothing much. I just wanted to see how you and Norma were doing, that's all."

"Oh, we're fine," Hank said. "Been keeping busy."

"Hank's been real busy," Norma said. "He and Wayne and Wilson cut down some trees at the meetinghouse yesterday."

That didn't take long.

"I wondered about that," Sam said. "I saw you walking through the field behind Panera carrying a chainsaw."

Norma turned back toward the sink, and Hank pointed to his head and made a circular motion, indicating Norma was a few bricks short of a sidewalk.

Norma turned back toward Hank. "I heard you and Wayne and Wilson talking about cutting down some trees at the meetinghouse. Don't you think it's time you let some of the younger men in the meeting do that?"

"Yes, you probably shouldn't be cutting down trees at the meetinghouse," Sam said. "It's made some people very upset."

"Remember when the trustees cut down a tree a few years ago and you were mad because you said it was the limb committee's job?" Norma said. "I hope you asked the limb committee before you cut down those trees yesterday."

"Yes, I hope you did, too," Sam said.

"I'm sure they won't mind," Hank said.

"Who's the clerk of the limb committee now?" Sam asked.

"I hope it isn't me," Norma said. "I never did like serving on that committee."

"No, it isn't you," Hank said. "It's Leonard Fink."

"Oh, my. Leonard isn't going to like you cutting down the trees," Norma said. "He doesn't like being left out."

"I bet Leonard won't be the only one upset," Sam said.

"Well, somebody had to do it," Hank blurted out. "We've got an addition that needs building and we can't sit around and wait on a bunch of bats."

"The lady from the DNR thinks I did it," Sam said. "And she thinks I killed the bats in the meetinghouse attic. She dug up half my backyard this morning, because she thinks I'm a serial killer. Do you know who might have killed the bats?"

"Don't look at me, I didn't touch them," Hank said. "I cut down the trees, yes, but I didn't kill any bats."

"Are you going to let the DNR know you cut down the trees?" Sam asked.

"Nope, it's none of their business," Hank said. "They're

our trees, I'm the clerk of the trustees, and am responsible for keeping our meetinghouse property safe. The trees were dying and had to go."

"Then I guess I'll have to tell them," Sam said.

"You can't do that," Hank said. "You're my pastor. I confessed something to you. You can't go blabbing it around to others."

"I don't know about that," Sam said. "I'm not quite sure that applies here."

"I designed a Catholic church once," Hank said. "I know all about this stuff. It's called the seal of the confessional. If I tell you something in confidence, you can't tell anyone else."

"We don't even have confessionals," Sam said. "And if we don't have confessionals, then we can't very well seal them, can we?"

"If people at meeting know I told you something in confidence and you betrayed that confidence, they'll never trust you with any of their secrets again," Hank said.

That was alarming. One of the reasons Sam had become a pastor was for the secrets. He loved nothing more than being in possession of a juicy bit of information no one else knew. Holding the secret close, then dribbling it out in small measures to a select audience, sworn to secrecy. It almost made up for the low pay.

"I won't say anything to the DNR," Sam said, giving in. "But I urge you to tell them what you did."

"Won't do it," Hank said. "It's our property, and my responsibility to maintain a safe environment."

Sam had to admire Hank. He'd been a pastor for over thirty years, thought he knew every trick in the book, but had been handily outsmarted by a lowly trustee.

He wondered if he could get Wilson and Wayne to spill their guts.

He hugged Norma good-bye, and she thanked him for stopping by and told him he was the best pastor they'd ever had, which would have felt nice, except she called him Stan.

Hank walked him to the door. "Let's see if we can't get moving on the addition now that the bats and trees are gone," Hank said. "Why don't you ask that DNR lady when we can start?"

"Since you're in charge of the trustees, I'll let you ask," Sam said, deftly dodging that unpleasant task and shifting it to Hank. That would teach him not to mess with a pastor.

57

⌒

In the few days Charles and Gloria Gardner had owned their tandem bicycle, they'd been inches from death a dozen times. Had they been aware of their near brushes, they would have been terrified. But with dimmed eyesight and diminished hearing, they pedaled happily onward, oblivious to the honking horns, the unseemly gestures, the screech of tires.

That morning, they woke early, ate breakfast, then pedaled fifteen miles to the nearest town, had lunch, got lost on their way home, and ended up twenty miles from Hope. They thought of calling Sam to come get them, then decided against it. He'd get all worked up and worried and drop hints that it was time to move to assisted living, which they most assuredly were not going to do. They stopped every couple of miles to ask someone directions, gradually making their way toward home. It was the most excitement they'd had in years, better than *Law & Order*.

"Sam ought to get himself and Barbara one of these," Charles Gardner said, pedaling along on a country road a few miles outside of town. "He's so uptight all the time. He needs to relax a bit."

"He's got a lot on his mind with this bat thing," Gloria said, in defense of their son.

"He needs to get over that. It's not like they're gonna throw him in jail."

"I guess he is a little uptight," Gloria said. "But he's always been that way. Too tense, always something on his mind."

Charles chuckled. "I knew a guy like that when I was in the army and we took him out and got him drunk."

"Oh, we can't do that. Sam's got enough of a problem with that."

Riding along, her mind lost in thought, she recalled having to help Barbara carry Sam into their house. She shuddered just thinking about it. What a day that had been. Sam was fortunate the members of the meeting hadn't found out about it. She'd been reading about ministers and alcoholism on the Internet and was amazed at what she'd discovered. Sam's denial only added to her worries. Denying they had a problem was the first thing alcoholics did. She worried the bats would put him over the edge, that he'd take up demon rum, lose his job, lose their home, lose his wife, and end up living on the street, or worse, living with them.

She had spoken to Roger about Sam, but he hadn't seemed all that concerned. He was distracted these days, having proposed to Christina Pringle and having to follow through with his proposal and actually commit himself to someone. He was thinking of drinking himself.

The memory of the day still haunted her. Narrowly escaping death at the hands of a texting little twit, then discovering her son had a drinking problem. Sometimes she wished the twit had killed her. Then Leonard and Wanda Fink showing up at the parsonage to borrow paper towels so they could clean the meetinghouse windows. She'd forgotten all about that. But the more she thought about it, the more surprised she was that Sam's drunkenness had remained a secret.

Something clicked in her mind. Wasn't that also the day the bats had been killed? Yes, she thought it was. It had to have been. She worked through the sequence of events. Getting hit by the twit, going to the hospital, Sam getting drunk, she and Barbara helping him into the parsonage, the Finks borrowing paper towels to clean the meetinghouse windows, Barbara putting Sam in the shower while she searched the garage for his secret stash of booze, her going home, eating supper, getting loopy on pain medicine, and going to the hospital the second time in one day.

The DNR lady had found the bag of bats early the next morning, the day after the Finks had cleaned the meetinghouse. It would have been like the Finks to kill a hundred and seven bats. She didn't know the Finks all that well, but what she did know, she didn't like. They didn't care for her son; they had made that abundantly clear, shooting down every suggestion he made at the church's monthly business meeting. Yes, the more she thought about it, the more guilty they seemed.

The problem with the Finks was that they'd never admit their guilt. They'd clam up. This wasn't like *Law & Order*, where they could find Leonard's DNA on the bats, or sweat him under the lights in a basement somewhere. She didn't even know where the Finks were. She'd phoned Wanda Fink the day before to see if she might take a turn in the nursery, but no one had answered, so she'd left a message. Wanda hadn't called back, which was unusual. Despite her general unpleasantness, she was good at returning phone calls. The Finks hadn't been at meeting on Sunday, something about boycotting worship since Bruno served wine. She thought that's what Sam had said. It occurred to her the Finks were on the lam, running from the law.

"Let's go by the Finks' house on our way home," she said to Charles. "I need to talk with Wanda about something."

"Why don't you just phone her?" Charles asked. He no more wanted to see the Finks than he wanted to jab a needle in his eye.

"I don't even think they're home. I just want to make sure."

They entered Hope on a back road, pedaled through town on the backstreets to the Finks' house. It was hard to miss, due to the sign in their yard that read *It Is Appointed Unto Men Once to Die, but After This the Judgment. Hebrews 9:27.* It had been in their yard for some time, a gift from the *Lester Hickam Revival Hour and Variety Show*, in gratitude for Leonard and Wanda's support. It had cost Lester Hickam four dollars to have made, and he mailed them out to anyone who donated at least five hundred dollars plus shipping and handling. It had been one of Lester's more successful fund-raisers, more successful even than the prayer cloths dampened by Lester's sweat, sweat he had worked up praying for his television family.

Gloria knocked on the Finks' front door with no result, looked in the backyard, then peered through the picture window into their living room, but saw no sign of life. Their mailbox was full, unread newspapers were lying on the driveway. She dialed their landline on her cell phone and listened to it ring unanswered inside their home.

"Looks like they left sometime on Sunday," Charles said, studying the newspapers. "Papers haven't been picked up since Monday morning."

"Just as I thought," Gloria said. "They've made their escape."

58

Gloria Gardner phoned Sam, who didn't pick up. His parents had been phoning a half-dozen times a day, usually when he was busy, about things they could figure out themselves if they put their minds to it. His father had called the night before at eleven o'clock to ask him who had the better price on toilet paper, Drooger's or Kroger.

"I'm just sitting here thinking about it," he'd told Sam.

Sitting where? Sam didn't want to know.

She phoned Sam again, and this time he answered.

"Have you been avoiding me?" she asked. "You never pick up the phone anymore."

"Did you call?" he asked, feigning innocence. "I must not have heard it ring."

"We're over at the Finks' house. You need to get over here."

"Does it have to be now? I'm right in the middle of something."

"Yes, right now."

He rolled up five minutes later to find his parents standing in the Finks' garage, nosing around.

"What are you doing in the Finks' garage? Where are they?"

"Not here," his father said. "They've hit the road."

"You shouldn't be in here," Sam said. "How did you get in here in the first place?"

"Popped the lock with a credit card," Charles Gardner said. "Saw it on *Law and Order*."

"Wanda and Leonard are the bat killers," his mother said.

"How do you know? Did they say so?"

"Heck, no, and they never will, but think about it," Gloria said. "They came to the door the day you were passed out drunk and asked to borrow some paper towels to clean the meetinghouse windows. The next thing you know, the bats are dead. I bet you dollars to doughnuts the Finks did it."

"I don't remember that," Sam said.

"Well, of course you don't," Gloria said. "You were drunker than a monkey."

"Are you sure they did it?" Sam asked.

"Who are the biggest sneaks in the church?" Gloria said.

"The Finks."

"Who's mean enough to kill an entire colony of bats and not blink an eye?" Gloria asked.

"The Finks."

"Who would happily not say a word about doing it, even if it meant you were wrongfully accused and sent to prison?" Gloria asked.

"Leonard and Wanda Fink," Sam concluded.

"There you have it."

"Maybe now you'll answer your phone when your mother calls you," Charles Gardner said.

"And there's one other thing that makes us suspect them," Gloria Gardner said.

"What's that?"

"A bag of bat poop," Charles Gardner said. "Look in that trash bag in front of the shelves."

Sam nudged the bag open with his foot. He'd never seen bat poop before, so took out his smartphone, went on Google, typed in the word *guano*, and studied the picture that popped up. Yep, it was bat poop. Pounds of it.

"That is disgusting," Sam said.

"Makes wonderful fertilizer," his father observed.

"Maybe we ought to take a picture of it so we can show it to the DNR," Sam said.

"That's a great idea, son. And while we're at it, we can mention we broke into their garage," Gloria said.

She loved her son, but he could be slow on the uptake.

"We take the picture, and we show it to the Finks to force a confession from them," Charles said.

They took out their smartphones and began snapping pictures.

"Hey, now that I think about it, I have the cell phone number of the DNR lady," Sam said. "It's on the business card she gave me. What if we buy a throwaway phone at Walmart, send her a picture of the poop along with the address where it can be found?"

Charles Gardner studied his son with a newfound respect. "That's a great idea. Why didn't I think of that?"

The phone cost fifty dollars, which Sam paid for in cash so they couldn't trace his credit card number. He hurried back to the Finks' house, took more poop pictures, and sent three of them to the DNR lady, along with the Finks' address and a cryptic message from Anonymous that she would find important evidence of a recent bat slaying in the garage at the aforementioned address. Then he removed the SIM card and battery from the phone, stomped all three parts to pieces, and tossed them in separate dumpsters on his way home.

It was the sneakiest thing he'd ever done as a pastor, probably even illegal, so he didn't tell Barbara.

It was disconcerting to know his parents could be so devious. Breaking and entering? Opening a door with a credit card? What had become of the saintly, albeit slightly irritating, parents he'd once known? Too much television, he decided. When this was all over, he'd have to speak with them about that.

59

↩

"I'm not sure that woman in the magazine was really hand-
less," Wanda Fink said out loud, somewhere around
Lexington, Kentucky, on their way home from Lester
Hickam's revival.

She'd been thinking about it ever since they'd left Dollywood, turning over the possibilities in her mind, and had
concluded that Lester Hickam was a fraud. It nearly killed
her to admit it, even to herself, after all the years of watching
Lester Hickam on Saturday nights. They had a lot of hours in-
vested in him, and quite a bit of money to boot. Somewhere
north of twenty thousand dollars, she figured, with only a
cheesy little yard sign to show for it.

She'd hinted at her suspicions to Leonard one night during
their trip and he'd blown up, telling her that Satan was de-
ceiving her, that she'd been hoodwinked by the mainstream
media, and that Brother Lester would no more cheat on Luella
than God would cheat on his wife, if God had a wife, which
Leonard wasn't sure about. They hadn't talked much since.
Just maintenance talk, like *Where do you want to eat?* and

Where's the toothpaste? and *Are you done with the catsup?*, until they hit the first Lexington exit on I-75 and Wanda couldn't contain herself any longer.

"I'm still not sure that woman in the magazine was really handless," she said.

"Here we go again," Leonard said. He'd been expecting just such a statement, and had his response ready. "Has Brother Lester ever lied to you?" he asked Wanda. "Has he ever looked you right in the eye, face-to-face, and told you something you knew to be untrue?"

Since she had never spoken to Brother Lester face-to-face, she had to concede that he had never personally lied to her.

"But you feel perfectly free to besmirch his reputation," Leonard said.

He shook his head, both amazed and disappointed.

"And this is why he's decided not to run for the presidency," Leonard said. "Because he wants to protect his wife from these kinds of attacks."

That had been the low point of the revival for Leonard, when Lester Hickam informed the congregation he wouldn't seek the presidency. Leonard had been hoping to ride Lester's coattails onto the school board, an unstoppable duo. Lester in the White House and Leonard on the school board. The arena had fallen silent after Lester's announcement, then the crying commenced. The men shouted "No," while the women wept. The men looked around, wildly, for someone to beat up—a reporter, perhaps, or a Democrat, or Muslim.

"Now listen, now listen," Brother Lester had said, gesturing for the crowd to be silent. "This doesn't mean we're giving up the fight. We still need your support. Yes, pray for us, we need your prayers. The battle isn't over. It is a battle for the world's soul and it needs the world's weapons. I don't like that it has come to that, but it has and we must be realistic. We need your financial gifts now more than ever."

Luella had cranked out the tears at that one.

"Look at what they've done to my wife," Lester thundered. "Defiled our marriage bed with their sick accusations, with their lies. Liberal media, big government, Christians under attack. Are we going to sit idly by and take it?"

Leonard thought of the dead bats and swelled with pride. He didn't care who knew it. How dare the government close their church! Let everyone else slink over to Bruno's with their tails between their legs. Not him. One hundred and seven dead bats, and he'd do it again, until the last bat in the world was dead, if that's what it took.

He wanted the world to know what he had done, to know true Christians weren't going to be bullied any longer. He rose from his seat and made his way forward to Brother Lester. Past the people in wheelchairs waiting for Lester to heal them. Past the blind, the deaf, the mute. Past the people Satan had attacked with head colds, flu, and sore knees, who needed delivery from their misery.

"Excuse me, excuse me," he said, winding his way through the people to the front of the line.

He climbed the stairs toward Brother Lester, calling out his name. Brother Lester turned, pausing in his preaching.

"I'm Leonard Fink."

Lester recognized the name immediately, having committed to memory the name of every giver over twenty thousand dollars.

Lester rushed toward him and embraced him, then introduced him to the arena.

It was a beautiful moment for Leonard, to stand arm in arm with Lester Hickam. A man who had stood with presidential candidates, a man who had taken on Satan single-handedly, a man who had sent the demons packing.

"We're under attack," Leonard said, speaking into Brother Lester's microphone. He launched into his story, the bats in the meetinghouse attic, the government shutting down their church, *shutting down God's house!*, and him killing the bats, dashing them upon the rocks. Well, not exactly, but Leonard liked the sound of it. It sounded very Old Testament.

The reaction was mixed. Some cheered, others were appalled. About fifty-fifty, which meant Leonard was probably costing him donations the longer he spoke. Brother Lester was nothing if not smooth. He eased the microphone from Leonard's hand, then began to pray that in this time of great tribulation, true Christians would be elected who would lead America back to God. He wept as he prayed, turning toward the camera so his tears could be seen. He'd want a picture of that for his next mailing. Tears were good for another fifty thousand dollars.

All the while he was nudging Leonard off the stage, trying to put distance between them, not wanting to be associated with the slaughter of bats, who weren't the most cherished of mammals, but people were funny about animals these days so it was best not to celebrate them being dashed upon the rocks.

Leonard ranted from Lexington to Louisville, seventy-five miles of fuming and seething.

"I tell you one thing I'm not going to sit still for," he raged. "I'm not going to stand by and let Sam Gardner turn our church into one of those gay churches. Those two women have got to go."

Wanda didn't respond. She had actually spoken to Chris and Kelly in the women's restroom two Sundays ago, just before worship. She had convinced herself she wouldn't like them, but Chris had complimented her outfit, something Leonard hadn't done in years, and Kelly had invited her to lunch later in the week. Wanda couldn't remember the last time someone had invited her out to eat. She'd declined Kelly's invitation, but listening to Leonard carry on, she was thinking she might call Kelly when they got home. She realized she didn't care what Chris and Kelly did in their bedroom. She thought about saying that to Leonard, halfway in between Lexington and Louisville, but decided against it. He was driving, after all, and she didn't want him to have a heart attack, crash, and die. At least not with her in the car.

60

~

W ell, I'll be darned," the husband of the DNR lady
said. "Would you come listen to this."

He'd been flipping through the channels, on his way to
ESPN, when he'd heard someone say something about bats
and big government and Christians being under attack.

"I think they're talking about you," he said to his wife,
whom he'd never considered to be the summation of all that
was wrong with America. A bit overeager at times, but other
than that a pretty good person.

"Can you back that up?" the DNR lady asked.

Her husband had spent thousands of dollars on a television
system that backed up, sped forward, skipped commercials,
and did everything but cook your breakfast.

He tapped a few buttons, and there was Leonard Fink, walking across the stage toward Lester Hickam.

"What'd he say his name was?" the DNR lady asked. "Back
that up, and slow it down."

They watched it again, in slow motion, with the sound
turned up.

"Sound likes he's saying 'Leonard Fink,'" her husband said.

"I saw him at the meetinghouse," she said. "Pause it. Right there."

She peered at the screen. "He's the janitor there. Why didn't I think of that?"

She hurried into their spare bedroom, where they kept their computer, went onto to the White Pages website, entered the name Leonard Fink, and saw seven entries appear on the screen. Six Leonard Funks and one Leonard Fink, of Hope, Indiana, residing at the very address texted to her by someone named Anonymous, along with a picture of bat poop.

She yelled back into the living room. "Can that television tell you when that show was recorded?" She wanted to make sure it wasn't a bat killing from years before.

"Says here it was filmed at their annual revival just two days ago in Chattanooga," he shouted back.

"Got him," she said triumphantly. Leonard Fink, the church janitor. She'd cracked the case. This would more than make up for ticketing the governor's brother for fishing without a license. Maybe now they'd even let her carry a Taser.

She phoned her supervisor, set up a meeting for the next morning, then outlined her next steps—the search warrant, the raid, filing the charges. She hoped Leonard Fink resisted arrest so she could crack him on the noggin a time or two. Let him know what it felt like to be smacked upside the head with a two-by-four. See how he liked it.

She yelled to her husband, "Can you record that segment on a flash drive?"

"Sure," he said, more than happy to justify all the money he'd spent on their television set.

She supposed she owed Sam Gardner an apology. She was so sure it had been him. He had fit the bat-killer profile. No, she wouldn't apologize yet. Maybe he hadn't killed the bats, but he probably had a hand in cutting down the trees. Maybe she needed another warrant to search his garage for a chainsaw. She wondered if trees had DNA, and whether she might find traces of the felled trees on his chainsaw. That would sink his boat. She imagined Leonard Fink and Sam Gardner sharing a prison cell for the next twenty years, getting roughed up in the showers, leaving prison old men. The thought delighted her.

61

"Are you going to the food pantry with me this week-end?" Barbara asked Sam as they were washing the supper dishes.

Sam mulled his options. If he said yes, he wouldn't be able to attend the pocketknife convention. He'd even talked Charley Riggle from the hardware store into going with him, which, if you thought about it, was kind of like a ministry, wooing the unsaved to Jesus via a pocketknife convention. If he said no to the food pantry, Barbara would forgive him, but not for a few days. She'd been suggesting lately that she did more work in the church than Sam did, which was probably true.

Then inspiration struck. "I was planning on working at the food pantry in the morning, then picking up Charley Riggle to go to the pocketknife convention in the afternoon. I'm real close to having him talked into coming to church, otherwise I'd spend the day at the food pantry."

Barbara bought it.

She phoned Chris and Kelly to tell them she and Sam would be able to help at the food pantry. They chatted about the meeting and its members. Chris mentioned that Ruby Hopper had brought her cousin Mary a pie, thanked her and Beth for visiting the meeting, and invited them back.

"It meant a lot to Mary," Chris said. "She and Beth were asked to leave their last church."

"That's sad," Barbara said. "How could you ask someone to leave church?"

Sam thought of several people he'd wanted to ask just that.

Barbara and Chris chatted a bit longer, just long enough for Sam to finish the dishes.

"What's on your agenda tonight?" Barbara asked Sam.

"I have a meeting with Wilson Roberts and Wayne Newby," Sam said. "They'll be here any minute now."

Barbara groaned. "I'll be so happy when we can use the meetinghouse again. What room will you be meeting in?"

"How about the screen room?" Sam said. "That way you can have the living room and kitchen."

"I don't have to feed them, do I?"

"I don't think so," Sam said. "I'm sure they will have eaten. They might want some coffee, though."

"Coffee, I can do."

Wayne and Wilson arrived just as the coffee was ready. Sam ushered them out to the screen room, Barbara poured them coffee, then excused herself.

"Thanks for coming over, guys," Sam began. "I really appreciate it."

Wayne and Wilson smiled. They had agreed Wilson would do the talking for them. Having owned a plumbing fixture empire, he had a way with words.

"It's always good to see you, Sam," Wilson said. "How can we help you?"

"I spoke with Hank yesterday and he told me you cut down those trees," Sam said.

"I knew it," Wayne screeched. "I knew he'd blame it on us. Didn't I tell you? I told you he'd try to pin it on us."

Wayne turned to Sam. "Hank's the one who did it. We didn't go anywhere near the trees. We stayed at the back edge of the property, while he went and did it. Isn't that right, Wilson?"

"That's right," Wilson said. "We didn't do anything. Hank did it all."

"I can't believe he told you," Wayne said. "We agreed not to tell anyone, and now he's gone and run his big mouth and everyone knows."

"No one knows but me," Sam said. "And he didn't tell me, Norma did. She overheard you talking."

It was some consolation to know Hank hadn't ratted them out.

"So now what do we do?" Sam asked.

"Do? We don't do anything," Wayne said. "I'm sure not telling anyone."

"Me, neither," Wilson said. "Our property. Our trees. We can do with them as we please."

"I think one of you needs to fess up, so we can wrap up this matter," Sam said. "Otherwise, we'll never get to build our addition. The DNR lady is pretty mad."

"I can live with the addition not being built," Wayne said. "It sure beats going to jail. How about you, Wilson?"

"Yeah, I can live without it."

Wayne looked at Sam. "You're not going to turn us in, are you?"

"He can't," Wilson said. "He's our pastor. We told him this in confidence. He can't say a word to anyone."

What was all this talk about pastoral confidentiality? Sam thought people watched too much television, shows about serial killers confessing heinous crimes to a priest, then went right on chopping up people while the priest agonized over whether or not to tip off the authorities. Sam would have spilled the beans in a heartbeat. He was half inclined to frogmarch Hank, Wayne, and Wilson down to the DNR lady and have them thrown in the pokey just to be done with this nonsense. What was the worst thing that could happen to him if he turned them in? It wasn't like anyone could arrest him. He might get chewed on by the meeting's elders, but that would be the extent of it. They'd spent three years searching for a pastor, and weren't likely to kick him to the curb for cooperating with the law. Still, one never knew what Quakers would do.

Times like this, he wished he could talk with a superintendent, but the current model was a knucklehead, who'd turned on Sam for accidentally marrying Chris and Kelly. How was he to know they'd been two women, with names like that? They hadn't even belonged to his church. They were Unitarians. Sam was called in at the last minute after the Unitarian pastor had fallen ill. He was a pinch-hitter, a last-minute substitution, and look what it had cost him.

"You need to get with Hank and decide what to do about this," Sam said. "You cut down the trees, not me. I'll tell you right now, if that DNR lady accuses me of doing it, I'm going to rat you out. It won't be a breach of confidence, either, since Norma's the one who told me, not you. It wasn't like you three came to me full of remorse to confess your sin."

"There was a time a man could come clean to his pastor without it being blabbed all over," Wilson said.

"Come on, Sam, take one for the team," Wayne said. "So

what if they think it's you. They're not going to throw a minister in jail."

"The heck they won't," Sam said. "It's against the law. I looked it up. A guy in Kentucky who killed bats got put in jail for eight months."

"If you confess to it, we'll pay for your lawyer," Wilson said. "We're too old to go to jail. We wouldn't last." His voice caught as he said it. He was nearly in tears. "We'll die in there."

Sam studied Wilson. He was right. They wouldn't last. A lifetime of ease had rendered them incapable of enduring hardship. The stress of the trial would kill them before they even went to jail. He wondered if Wayne was right when he said they wouldn't throw a minister in jail. People were funny about ministers. Every time he'd been pulled over by a police officer, he'd mentioned he was a pastor and they'd let him go with a warning.

"Let me see what I can do," Sam said. "I'll talk with the DNR lady. Maybe if she finds out who killed the bats in the attic, that will satisfy them."

The thought of Leonard Fink going to jail didn't bother Sam in the least.

What a mess this was turning out to be. A congregation full of outlaws, most of his trustees headed to jail if he didn't do something.

He walked Wayne and Wilson to the door, said good-bye, then returned to the screen room to think. He was starting to feel bad for tipping off the DNR lady about Leonard. Maybe he shouldn't have done that. He was Leonard's pastor, after all. What kind of pastor had one of his parishioners arrested? What had he become?

62

Sam didn't sleep well. He dreamed he'd been fired and he and Barbara were living with his parents, slowly going mad. Barbara's alarm clock sounded, waking him. He ate breakfast, took a long bath, and still groggy, phoned Ruby Hopper, who was awake and chipper and happy for Sam to come over.

He walked to her house, hoping the exercise would energize him. She was seated on her front porch, waiting for him. It was a warm morning, a hint of summer in the air. She offered Sam her rocking chair and took a seat in her porch swing.

"What brings you out this fine morning?" she asked.

"We've got problems," he said.

"Oh?"

"Leonard Fink killed the bats, and Hank, Wilson, and Wayne cut down the two trees."

"What two trees?"

"The two trees in the way of our new addition. The trees the bats were in. They cut them down."

"Oh, my, what were they thinking?" Ruby asked.

"They weren't thinking."

"When did this happen?"

"The night before last," Sam said. "I found out yesterday. I went to visit Hank and Norma, and Norma told me. Then last night I met with Wayne and Wilson and they want me to confess to doing it. They don't think the DNR would put a minister in jail."

"Well, you're not going to do that," Ruby Hopper said. "I can't believe they would even ask such a thing. Now, what is this you said about Leonard killing the bats?"

"Apparently, the day the bats were killed, Leonard and Wanda went in the meetinghouse to clean the windows. They must have seen the bats and killed them."

"How do we know that?"

"We found a bag of bat guano in their garage," Sam said.

"Who is 'we'?"

"Uh, my mom, dad, and me."

"What were you doing in their garage? I thought the Finks were on vacation. I phoned Wanda to see if she wanted to serve on the pie committee next year, and she told me they were in Tennessee. Are they back?"

"They might be now," Sam said. "But they weren't yester-day afternoon."

"Then how did you get in their garage?"

"My dad unlocked the door using a credit card. He saw it on television."

Ruby shook her head in disbelief.

"So our janitor is a bat killer, our pastor and his parents broke into someone's house, and our trustees, in violation of the law, knowingly eradicated the habitat of an endangered species."

"Yep, that pretty well sums it up," Sam said.

"Does the DNR know any of this?"

"They know about Leonard," Sam said.

"How did they find out?"

Sam could barely bring himself to answer.

"I went to Walmart, bought a phone, took a picture of the bat poop, and texted it along with Leonard's address to the DNR lady. Then I smashed the phone and threw it away," Sam said. "I saw it on TV."

Saying it out loud like that made Sam feel horrible.

"Oh, Lord, we get a little money and it ruins us. Look what we've become," Ruby said.

Sam's phone buzzed in his pocket. He pulled it out and checked the screen. It was the DNR lady. No sense avoiding her. The damage was done. It was time to come clean. He answered the phone.

"Is this Sam Gardner?"

"Yes."

"Do you know a Mr. Leonard Fink?"

"Yes," Sam said. "He's a member of our meeting. He and his wife serve as our janitors."

"We're at their house now. They returned home last evening from a vacation. We received an anonymous tip about a bag of bat guano in their garage."

Sam wanted to vomit. He could hear Wanda weeping in the background. How could he have done this?

"It seems Mr. Fink appeared on a, let me see here, I've forgotten this guy's name"—Sam could hear the rustle of paper—"here it is, a Reverend Lester Hickam's television show and admitted to killing the bats. We have the whole thing on tape."

Sam felt a little better, hearing that.

"Yes, he seems quite proud of himself. He says he acted alone, that no one helped him. He's admitting to everything."

"Are you arresting him?" Sam asked.

"We most certainly are. He has violated the Endangered Species Act."

"I'll be there in just a few minutes," Sam said. "Can you give me time to see him?"

"Sure, I'm in no hurry."

Ruby went with him. They drove Ruby's car, and arrived at the Finks' home five minutes later. They found Wanda and Leonard in their living room. Wanda was sobbing. Leonard was stoic, a martyr for his faith, standing firm against big government. Ruby sat next to Wanda to console her. Sam wasn't sure what to do, so stood next to Leonard, who seemed to think Jesus would descend on the clouds any moment with a battalion of angels to smite the DNR lady. The DNR lady was talking on her phone, looking peeved. She hung up after a few minutes.

"I guess I don't get to put you in jail after all," she said. "You're too old. My boss said to come down to the office so we can file charges and take your mug shot and start the paperwork, but then we'll release you on your own recognizance. He doesn't think you'll go anywhere. He doesn't even want me to handcuff you." She sounded thoroughly disappointed.

"Should we get a lawyer?" Wanda asked.

"I certainly would," the DNR lady said.

"Stacey Maxwell is a lawyer," Sam said. "Maybe she could help."

"Time to go," the DNR lady said.

They walked Leonard out. It didn't look like any arrest

they'd ever seen on television. They even let him drive his own car to the DNR office.

Ruby and Sam stayed with Wanda, eventually wandering out to the garage, where another DNR officer was bagging the guano for evidence.

"Say," Ruby asked him, "you don't suppose when you're done with that, I could have some for my garden?"

63

Ruby stayed with Wanda, and Sam caught a ride home with a DNR officer. He phoned Wayne, Wilson, and Hank, summoning them to his house. They arrived within fifteen minutes and assembled in his living room.

"Leonard Fink has been arrested for killing the bats," he told them.

When they thought about it, they weren't surprised.

"We should have known that," Wilson said. "Him being the janitor and in there all the time."

"Quite frankly, we thought it was you and your dad," Wayne said.

"I wouldn't do that," Sam said. "What kind of person do you think I am?"

"So how'd they catch Leonard?" Hank asked.

Sam didn't mention texting a tip to the DNR lady.

"He went on television and admitted to it," Sam said. "Apparently, the DNR lady saw it, got a search warrant, and found a bag of bat guano in their garage."

"It's great for roses," Wilson said.

"Maybe we can pin the trees on Leonard," Wayne said.

"We can't do that," Sam said. "What are you thinking?"

"He's already in trouble. What's a few more months in jail?"

"I would advise you three to hire an attorney and come clean," Sam said. "And the sooner, the better."

"I guess this means you're not going to help us by saying you did it," Wilson said.

"No, I'm not going to do that."

"Isn't that Maxwell woman a lawyer?" Hank asked. "That new lady whose husband works for the Colts."

"Yes, she is," said Sam.

"Maybe she'll help us for free, since it's for the church," Wayne said.

"But it isn't for the church," Sam said. "You weren't acting on the church's behalf."

"She doesn't need to know that," Hank said.

"There have been enough lies," Sam said. "From now on it's all the truth, all the time."

"Can you call her for us, Sam? We barely know her," Wilson said.

They met that evening, after Herb got home to watch the babies. Stacey Maxwell, Sam, Ruby Hopper, and the three offenders, who by then were worked into a tizzy, having spent the day mulling over the horrors of prison life.

They spared no detail, revealing everything they had done, down to the last disgusting detail. Sam didn't mention texting the bat guano picture to the DNR lady. There was really no need to.

"So let me get this right. You cut down two trees that harbored Indiana bats, a federally protected species, after you'd been ordered by the DNR to leave them alone?" Stacey asked.

"Technically, Hank cut them down," Wilson said. "Wayne and I just went along to keep him company."

"But you knew about it, and went to the meetinghouse yard with him?"

"Not quite. We pretty much waited for him in the field behind Panera," Wayne said. "I don't even think we went on the meetinghouse property."

"It doesn't matter," Stacey explained. "You knew he was going to do it. You went along with him. Under the law, you're just as guilty."

She turned to Sam. "Did you know they were going to do this?"

"Absolutely not."

"Who else knows about this?" Stacey asked.

"My wife," Hank said.

"And my wife," Sam said. "I tell her everything."

"Sam told me this morning," Ruby Hopper said. "I mentioned it to Wanda Fink. I suppose she'll say something to Leonard."

"I said something to Doreen," Wayne said.

"I took my chainsaw to Riggle's Hardware to have it sharpened," Hank said. "I might have mentioned it to Charley."

"As long as we're being honest," Wilson said. "I think I told a few of my friends in Rotary. They wanted to know why I'd missed our Rotary meeting that night."

"I think the cashier at Panera heard us talking about it," Wayne said. "Remember that, Wilson?"

Stacey sighed.

"We need to get out in front of this," she said. "If we confess before they find out, it'll look a lot better for you. Do you agree?"

"I thought we were protected by the First Amendment," Hank said. "Doesn't that give us the freedom to practice our religion?"

"It most certainly does," Stacey said. "And if you can prove that cutting down a tree to displace a bat colony is part of your religion, then we might have a case. Otherwise, I suggest you confess, and the sooner the better."

64

Leonard Fink had never been in trouble with the law. He'd spent most of the day at the DNR office, arriving home well after supper. Jesus hadn't descended on the clouds to help him, which was something of a disappointment considering all he'd done for Jesus. They'd advised him not to say anything until they'd appointed an attorney to help him, but he ignored their advice, made a statement, signed a confession, and was charged with violating the Endangered Species Act.

The DNR lady was concerned. Something about Leonard Fink didn't feel quite right. He seemed a little crazy, a half bubble off center. She began to worry he would be ruled insane, and set free to kill all the bats he wanted. Geez, it was crazy. You could practically barbecue a bald eagle and nothing would happen to you. She was beginning to wish she'd dragged Leonard Fink behind the house when he'd first confessed, pounded him a time or two with a two-by-four, and let it go at that.

His confession was anticlimactic. She'd wanted the chance

to break him down, confront him with the evidence, yell and scream a bit. Instead, he'd folded within thirty seconds of their arrival. She'd knocked on the door, stuck her badge in his face, and he'd said, "I knew you'd find me. I did it. I killed them. A hundred and seven bats. It was me."

She'd wanted to arrest Wanda as an accessory, but her boss had refused. He was too soft. Wanda had known everything, hadn't reported it, and was going to get off scot-free. There was no justice anymore.

Leonard was allowed to make one phone call, which he used to call Lester Hickam in Chattanooga, who promised to say a prayer for him. Leonard asked if maybe he could send a lawyer up to Indiana to defend him. Lester promised to look into it, then said he was busy and couldn't talk any longer. Leonard heard giggling in the background.

The DNR lady brought him Chinese for lunch, from a take-out down the street, a kindness he hadn't expected. He broke open a fortune cookie and pulled out a piece of paper. *Exciting things are happening today.* They had that right.

He was starting to wish he hadn't killed the bats. It had seemed like the thing to do at the time. When he was a kid, his father had killed bats right and left, with tennis rackets, frying pans, and Ping-Pong paddles. You saw a bat, you killed it. Otherwise, they got in your hair and bit your neck and you died a week later from rabies. He thought he'd been doing the meeting a favor.

He was beginning to suspect that spilling his guts on national television wasn't the brightest idea. Or keeping the guano. He should have pitched the poop and kept his trap shut. Now he was headed to jail, where he would meet up with an animal-rights gang who would catch him in some lonely

240 •   Philip Gulley

corner of the prison yard and do unspeakable things to his person. It wasn't the retirement he'd imagined.

And poor Wanda. She hadn't deserved any of this. He'd spent the entire trip home railing at her, getting worked up, worried sick, and taking it all out on her. He wouldn't blame her if she left him. He wished he'd used his one phone call to talk with her and tell her he was sorry. He wondered if he'd ever see her again. What if they tossed him in Guantanamo Bay and no one ever heard from him again?

Supper was Chinese again, another fortune cookie, *Things are looking up*, then the DNR lady came in a little after nine and told him he could go. She ordered him not to leave town, then attached a device to his ankle that she said would electrocute him if he drove beyond the town limits.

"It's like a shock collar that dogs wear, except it's more powerful. You cross the town limits and it shocks you automatically. It'll beep before it kills you, and you'll have thirty seconds to get back inside the town limits."

It was an old coyote tracking collar she'd had lying around in her desk for a couple of years, but Leonard didn't need to know that.

She almost felt sorry for him.

Sam, Ruby Hopper, and that new lady from meeting, Stacey something, were visiting with Wanda when he arrived home. The day's trauma had taken most of the stupid out of him, so he didn't argue or bicker or preach. He hugged Wanda and apologized and told her he loved her, then sat in his recliner, his hands covering his eyes. He sat silently for a few moments, then spoke.

"I called Lester Hickam to ask for a lawyer, but I don't think he's going to send one. I heard a woman in the background. I don't think it was Luella," Leonard said.

"That man's a fraud," Wanda said. "He's not getting a dime more of our money."

"That's why we're here," Sam said. "As you know, Stacey is an attorney. She has agreed, as a favor to the meeting, to help you and several others who've been caught up in this mess."

"What others?" Leonard asked.

Sam debated whether he could trust Leonard with the names, then decided the time had come to be completely forthright. Except about the text he'd sent the DNR lady. They didn't need to know that. There was no point in complicating matters.

"Hank Withers, Wayne Newby, and Wilson Roberts cut down the two trees that were in the way of the addition," Sam said.

"To be more precise, Hank Withers did it," Ruby said. "But Wayne and Wilson knew about it and went with him."

"What I'd like to do is approach the DNR with all four of you, and see if we can't get them to agree to a settlement that would keep you out of jail," Stacey Maxwell said. "Given your ages and the situation, I think they might be amenable to some type of arrangement. Of course, the prosecutor's office must agree to it, also."

"I wouldn't have to go to jail?" Leonard asked.

"We'll do all we can to keep you out," Stacey said.

"Why are you doing this for us?" Wanda asked.

"Well, Sam explained the situation to me, we attend the same church, and I'm an attorney and want to be useful. Plus, I'm bored just sitting at home watching Emma and Ezra."

The Finks had made such little room for grace in their lives, they were perplexed by its presence. They didn't say anything, just bowed their heads and sniffed.

242 • Philip Gulley

"We can't afford much," Leonard said finally. "But we'll pay you what we can."

"I was thinking you could watch the babies whenever I worked on this," Stacey said.

"We'd be happy to do that," Wanda said, though slightly mystified why anyone would do anything for free, having grown accustomed to Lester Hickam and his type milking folks for every dollar they could.

Then Leonard and Wanda Fink, so deeply moved by the kindness of someone they scarcely knew, began to weep.

"Yes, we'd be happy to watch your children anytime," Leonard said, sniffing and snorting. "Anytime at all."

65

~~

The next day was Saturday. Sam and Barbara were up by seven, showered, ate, and at eight o'clock were passing out groceries to needy people at the food pantry. A good percentage of Hope Meeting was there, working side by side, with the exception of the criminals, who remained at home contemplating their sins. The meeting's lesbian contingent, now numbering four, unless an unknown lesbian were deep in the closet and wished to remain there, were directing the efforts, seasoned hands in the food pantry ministry. They were done by eleven, the shelves bare, the food distributed, ready for more food to be gathered in for the next Saturday.

Sam was elated. He could still make it back to Hope, eat lunch with Barbara, and be at Riggle's Hardware at noon to pick up Charley and head to the pocketknife convention guilt-free. The convention consisted mostly of middle-aged white guys with large stomachs trading pocketknives with one another. Most of the men wore T-shirts touting gun companies. It made Sam feel uneasy, and he hoped they didn't discover he was a pacifist and kill him. Charley was the only one who knew he was Quaker, but he didn't tell anyone else, so Sam survived the convention and even managed to trade two of his newer knives for an older, rarer model.

On the drive home, Sam swore Charley to secrecy, then told him about Leonard killing the bats.

"Yes, I knew all about that," Charley admitted.

"How did you?" Sam asked. "We just now found out."

"Leonard came in and bought caulk to plug up the cracks where the bats had come in."

"I sure wish you had mentioned that to me," Sam said. "It would have saved us a lot of trouble. For a while there the DNR thought I had done it."

"I have a code," Charley said. "A hardware man can't go blabbing about his customer's purchases. It's a violation of confidentiality. How would you like it if I told everyone about you rewiring that outlet last month and almost burning the parsonage down?"

Sam supposed he wouldn't care for that.

Then, since he was tired of keeping secrets, he told Charley about Hank, Wilson, and Wayne cutting down the two trees full of bats.

"Knew about that, too," Charley said. "I sharpened Hank's chainsaw the Saturday before and he told me then what he was going to do."

"You know, you might tell me these things in advance," Sam suggested. "That way I can intervene and keep them from happening."

"Can't," Charley said. "It would be a violation of a—"

"I know, I know. A violation of a confidence."

"You got it," Charley Riggle said. "I will tell you one thing, though."

"What's that?"

"Your father has a floor sander reserved for all next week. He said you've agreed to sand all his floors. Just thought you'd want to know."

Sam sighed.

"I actually made no such promise."

"Well, don't tell him I told you," Charley said.

"So if I invited you to church, would you come?" Sam asked, remembering the professed reason for attending the pocketknife convention with Charley.

"No, I don't think so," Charley said. "You Quakers seem a little too wacky for me. I like my church to be calm."

"Not everyone's wacky," Sam said. "A bunch of us spent the morning helping at a food pantry."

"Yep, knew that, too. Kelly mentioned it to me yesterday when she came in and bought a new heating element for a water heater," Charley said. "She really knows her way around a hardware store."

"You know she's a lesbian, don't you?"

"No, but what's that got to do with it?" Charley asked.

"Oh, you know, lesbians are good at those kinds of things," Sam said.

It sounded ignorant even as he said it, like saying Polish people were better polka dancers. He wished he hadn't said it.

"I'm not sure about that," Charley said. "I've known lots of women good at home maintenance who weren't lesbians. But I tell you what I think is interesting."

"What's that?" Sam asked.

"I think it's interesting that the one lady in your church with the most enthusiasm for Christian service is a lesbian who is new to the congregation, and the people killing bats and squabbling over money are the longtime members."

That was interesting, and more than a little depressing, implying as it did that long-term exposure to Christian community had a negative effect.

"Then again, maybe I'm just sympathetic toward lesbians. I kind of know what it feels like to be one," Charley said.

"Oh?"

"Yep, I've always been attracted to women, too."

Sam chuckled.

"They can be pretty nifty," he agreed.

66

The Friends of Hope met at Bruno's the next morning for worship, being too afraid to ask the DNR lady if they could have their meetinghouse back. Sam didn't think it was his job to ask anyway. The trustees had got them in this mess, let them ask.

The Finks were there, trying their best to fade into the background. They stayed in the nursery, or the closest thing Bruno had to one, a far corner of the restaurant where they'd rolled out a rug and scattered a few rubber toys for the babies to chew on.

They bumped Norma from the electronic keyboard, downloaded piano music to Sam's smartphone, and struggled through the first hymn, followed by joys and concerns, Sam's favorite part of worship, unless someone went on and on about their ailments, which Wilson Roberts tended to do, droning on about various aches and pains, all of which could have been avoided if he had dropped fifty or sixty pounds. But he was subdued this morning, chastened by his crimes.

Kelly thanked everyone who had helped at the food pantry

the day before, then Stacey Maxwell stood and announced that her dog bite was healing nicely. Ruby Hopper reported that the bat killer had been caught, didn't give a name, but asked the meeting to pray for him, that he would draw closer to the Lord and become a contributing member of society.

"So if there's a fine, is Leonard going to pay it, or will the meeting pay it?" Wayne Newby asked. "Because technically he was working for the church when he killed them, but we didn't tell him to kill them. I could see it going either way."

"We'll discuss that at our next business meeting," Ruby said diplomatically.

"As for those trees," Wayne continued, "that was Hank's doing. Wilson and I didn't set foot on the meeting's property. It was all Hank's idea."

"Let's not discuss this during worship," Ruby suggested.

There were several visitors that morning, all of them watching on, fascinated.

"When do we get our meetinghouse back?" Hank Withers asked.

"Please, friends, let's hold off this conversation until our next business meeting," Ruby said.

"You're welcome to worship here as long as you want," Bruno called out from behind the counter. The Sunday before had been one of his most profitable Sundays ever. "Don't forget the ten percent discount for anyone who stays for Sunday dinner."

Sam was desperate to get worship back on track, so stood, thanked people for sharing, and launched into a prayer, asking God to do first one thing and then another, as if God were not wise enough to discern these needs without Sam's help.

Then he delivered his sermon, continuing the series on

church history, but skipping nearly 1,400 years, jumping from the Council of Jerusalem to the founding of Quakerism, sparing the congregation scores of sermons on topics of little interest to them. At this rate, he'd be done with the series in another month, two at the most, and could move on to more interesting matters.

After the sermon, they settled into silence, sang a closing song, then Bruno brought out dessert. People lingered to visit. Sam sought out the visitors, welcoming them to the meeting and inviting them to return. They had questions about the bats, which Sam answered, avoiding the more gruesome details.

Out of the corner of his eye, he noticed Stacey Maxwell gathering Leonard, Hank, Wayne, and Wilson at a table in the back corner. She caught his eyes and gestured for him to join them.

When they were seated, she said, "I want to approach the DNR tomorrow to see if they might be interested in a settlement."

"You mean money," Wayne said. "We're going to give them money?"

"It's that or jail," Stacey said. "Take your pick."

"How much are we talking?" Wayne asked.

"The maximum fine for violating the Protected Species Act is $50,000 per episode," Stacey explained. "But I'm going to start low and offer $5,000, along with an offer to install bat houses on the meetinghouse property to expand the bat's habitat. Just so you understand, that's a $2,500 offer from Leonard for killing the bats and a $2,500 offer from the other three for cutting down the trees."

Leonard suggested they divide the fine four ways, so that all the guilty parties paid the same amount. Better yet, he thought the meeting paying the fine would be a wonderful example of Christians bearing one another's burdens, as instructed by the Apostle Paul in the book of Galatians, chapter six, verse two.

Wayne and Wilson felt little need to serve as an example for anything and informed Leonard and Hank they were on their own, fine-wise.

Stacey headed them off at the pass by changing the subject.

"Leonard, if you and Wanda can be at my house tomorrow morning at nine, I'll have my initial meeting with the DNR."

"I'll go with you," Hank Withers said. "I'm pretty good at negotiating. I was an architect, you know."

"Thank you, but no. I want to approach them by myself. Besides, if you come with me, they might deduce that you're the one who cut down the trees. Right now, I want to keep names out of it."

Smooth, Sam thought. He made a mental note to hire Stacey if he ever ran afoul of the law.

"Now, at some point they will want to know your names. But before we get to that point, I need to know if any of you have a criminal history. I want to be able to tell them you've never been in trouble with the law."

She eyed each man separately. "No prior arrests? Nothing that will come back and bite us if I tell them you're all upstanding citizens who've never been in trouble."

Leonard Fink shifted in his chair. "Uh, how far back will they look?"

"I assume back to when you turned eighteen," Stacey said.

He breathed a sigh of relief. "We're good to go then."

"What did you do, Leonard?" Wayne Newby asked. "Steal something? Murder someone?"

"Yep, someone was poking his nose in my business, so I killed him," Leonard said.

Stacey ordered them not to do anything stupid between now and the next day, reminded Leonard to be at her house the next morning at nine, then dismissed them. Sam hung back to speak with her.

"So what kind of chances do you think they have?" he asked.

"It's hard to say. It all depends on what kind of mood the DNR is in. Their age will certainly work in their favor. Judges don't like sending old men to jail. Especially first-time offenders."

"I hope they avoid jail," Sam said, thinking how busy his life would become if four of his church members were imprisoned and he had to visit them each week, plus visit their wives, plus make sure their lawns got mowed.

Yes, jail would be an absolute disaster.

67

The DNR lady woke up Monday morning depressed, feeling the same way she had after ticketing the governor's brother. Something was amiss, she could sense it. Leonard Fink was going to walk. For several weeks she had harbored the hope that the bat killer would be sentenced to the electric chair, sending a clear message that cruelty to living things would not be tolerated.

She had overheard the big man, the director himself, on the phone, speaking to someone in the governor's office. The director was a political appointee who had donated five thousand dollars to the governor's reelection campaign and in turn had been given a job that pulled in something north of a hundred thousand dollars a year.

"You might point out to the governor that bats aren't like puppies. If the DNR cracks down on this guy, the church people aren't going to like it. We've already shut down their church. I'm not even sure we had the authority to do that. But this Fink guy has already been on one television show and he might be going on others. These people buy television time by the hour. This is going to come back and bite us, I promise you that. I'd find a way to drop this matter, and quick."

All that work for nothing. Finding the bats. Sorting the bats. Closing the church. Digging up the pastor's yard. Securing the search warrants. Searching Leonard Fink's house. Finding the bat poop. Filing charges. Arresting Leonard Fink. All for nothing.

When she arrived at work, a note was on her blotter instructing her to see the director. She knew what was coming.

He was livid. "You shut down the church? Who told you to do that? Those people have been meeting in that church for years without hurting those bats. If you'd have just left them alone, those bats would have been fine." He was shouting by now. "I want you to call that pastor and apologize, and you better hope to God they don't go to the newspapers with this, or heads will roll around here and yours will be first. Get rid of the paperwork, get rid of the evidence. Now!"

She decided to tell Sam in person, and phoned him, asking him to meet her at Leonard's house. She stopped by her desk, trashed her paperwork, deleted the file from her computer, went to the evidence room and retrieved the bag of bat poop she had seized from Leonard's garage, then drove the twenty minutes out to Hope.

Sam, Leonard, Wanda, and some woman with two babies were waiting on the Finks' front porch.

"It's your lucky day," she told Leonard. "The governor doesn't want to have charges filed against you."

She turned to Sam. "You can have your church back."

She stared at Stacey Maxwell. "Who are you?"

"A friend of the family," Stacey said.

"I'm not going to jail?" Leonard asked, sensing a glimmer

254 • Philip Gulley

of hope in what had been a dark and threatening day. "It's all over?"

"It's over as far as you're concerned," the DNR lady said.

"What about the trees being cut down?" Stacey asked.

"What about them? They're your trees."

"I'm sorry for killing the bats," Leonard said. "I'll never do it again."

That helped. The DNR lady softened.

"Do you want your bat poop back?" she asked.

"I don't ever want to see anything having to do with bats for the rest of my life," Leonard said.

"Just one favor," the DNR lady said. "The governor would appreciate it if you didn't say anything to the TV and newspaper folks. He wants to keep this quiet."

"Not a word," Leonard promised. "Not one single word."

The parking garage for the DNR was next to the state office building. The DNR lady had driven in and out of it a thousand times over her ten-year career, so knew the exact place the DNR director parked. What a fathead. He drove a convertible with a Ducks Unlimited license plate, number one. What kind of moron went around blasting ducks out of the air on the weekends and headed up the Department of Natural Resources on the weekdays? Politicians. She couldn't stand them.

It was a gorgeous late spring day. The sky was blue, the top was down on the director's convertible, and the poop was solid, tumbling out of the bag and over the convertible seats, filling the nooks and crannies. He'd be vacuuming it out for years.

68

ank Withers wanted to sue the state for delaying their building project.

"It's gonna cost us about two hundred thousand more than we have, if we do it right. Let's threaten to sue them for a million dollars and see if they'll settle for two hundred thousand," he told Sam.

"We'll do no such thing," Sam said.

Wayne Newby was beside himself with joy. No fine, no going to prison and having unspeakable things done to him.

Wilson Roberts was so pleased he promised to pay for bat houses just the same. A dozen of them, along the edge of the woods, bat condominiums. Plus, he vowed to personally donate, in the name of Hope Friends Meeting, ten thousand dollars to Save the Bats!

Sam phoned his parents to report the happy news. They invited him and Barbara over for dinner that evening to celebrate. His father wanted to ask him a question. Nothing big. Just a small favor, a little something. Would six o'clock work?

Sam and Barbara walked the three blocks to his parents' house. He hoped they were having fried chicken. Barbara had stopped frying their food several years before, and Sam was craving lard. Stepping through the front door, the smell of chicken filled the air. Ambrosia. It was as if the Triune God had woken that morning determined to bless Sam Gardner. Not only had his flock avoided prison, his mother had prepared fried chicken, mashed potatoes, green beans, and wait for it, she said, close your eyes, think of your favorite thing in the whole wide world.

He thought of his wife and his sons and pocketknives. He thought of Hope Meeting and all his friends and their screen room in the summer and their fireplace in the winter.

"Too many favorite things," he said to his mother. "I can't think of just one."

"Did you think of homemade ice cream?" she asked. "With strawberries?"

Ecstasy.

"Your father made it," Gloria Gardner said. "He's going to ask you to sand the floors this week. Just thought I'd warn you."

The fried chicken was just as he remembered. Crispy on the outside, juicy on the inside.

"Well, that's great news about the DNR not pressing charges," Charles Gardner said, pushing back from the supper table. "I guess that means you're not going to be quite as busy as you thought you were."

"Oh, I've still got plenty to do," Sam said.

"I was hoping maybe you could give me a few hours this week. I've rented a floor sander from Riggle's Hardware and might need a hand sanding the floors."

"I don't know, Dad. I'm pretty busy this week."

"You know, one day I'll be dead and you'll give anything to spend time with me sanding floors," Charles Gardner said.

"Ah, the old one-day-I'll-be-dead argument," Sam said.

It was a favorite ploy of his father's, begun when Sam was a teenager whenever his father wanted something from him.

You know, one day I'll be dead and you'll give anything to mow the lawn one more time for me.

You know, one day I'll be dead and you'll give anything to be able to clean the gutters one more time.

You know, one day I'll be dead and you'll give anything to let me have that last chicken leg.

The one-day-I'll-be-dead argument made little sense, but it was highly effective.

"Let me look at my schedule," Sam said. "No promises. But I'll see what I can do."

"That's great. And just because I knew you would, I went ahead and made your favorite dessert, homemade ice cream with strawberries. My way of thanking you."

He hurried into the kitchen to retrieve the ice cream, then carried it into the dining room.

"Hey, there's my Tupperware bowl," Barbara said. "I wondered where it went."

"You brought a salad here in it, honey," Gloria Gardner said. "Remember?"

"No, but that's okay. I'm just glad to have it back."

"You know, Dad, I'm kind of full," Sam said. "I think I'll pass on the ice cream."

"Nonsense. Just have a little," he said, spooning out two large scoops of ice cream from the Tupperware bowl onto Sam's plate.

Sam thought it tasted a little like rabbit, which he had heard tasted like chicken. He heaped on more strawberries.

They stayed another half hour, then excused themselves and walked home. Sam was carrying the Tupperware bowl full of leftover ice cream.

"Did that ice cream taste a little funny to you?" Barbara asked.

"It was the chicken," Sam said. "I read an article about it once. If you eat ice cream after chicken, the ice cream tastes like chicken."

Barbara smiled at Sam. "You know the most interesting things."

She reached around and stuck her hand in his back pocket.

"It just goes to show you're never too old to stop learning," Sam said.

"You've got that right," Barbara said. "You've got that absolutely right."